LOITERING WITH INTENT

MURIEL SPARK

Loitering With Intent

COWARD, McCANN & GEOGHEGAN

NEW YORK

The quotations from the *Life* of Benvenuto Cellini are
gratefully taken from Miss Anne Macdonell's
translation in the Everyman edition.

Library of Congress Cataloging in Publication Data

Spark, Muriel.
    Loitering with intent.

    I. Title.
PR6037.P29L6   1981   823'.914   80-26049
ISBN 0-698-11047-1

LOITERING WITH INTENT

Chapter One

One day in the middle of the twentieth century I sat in an old graveyard which had not yet been demolished, in the Kensington area of London, when a young policeman stepped off the path and came over to me. He was shy and smiling, he might have been coming over the grass to ask me for a game of tennis. He only wanted to know what I was doing but plainly he didn't like to ask. I told him I was writing a poem, and offered him a sandwich which he refused as he had just had his dinner, himself. He stopped to talk awhile, then he said good-bye, the graves must be very old, and that he wished me good luck and that it was nice to speak to somebody.

This was the last day of a whole chunk of my life but I didn't know that at the time. I sat on the stone slab of some Victorian grave writing my poem as long as the sun lasted. I lived nearby in a bed-sitting-room with a gas fire and a gas ring operated by pre-decimal pennies and shillings in the slot, whichever you preferred or had. My morale was high. I needed a job, but that, which should have been a depressing factor when viewed in cold blood, in fact simply was not. Neither was the swinishness of my landlord, a Mr. Alexander, short of stature. I was reluctant to go home lest he should waylay me. I owed him no rent but he kept insisting that I should take a larger and more expensive room in his house, seeing that I had overcrowded the small single room with my books, my papers, my boxes and bags, my food-stores and the evidence of constant visitors who stayed to tea or came late.

So far I had stood up to the landlord's claim that I was virtually living a double-room life for single-room pay. At the same time I was fascinated by his swinishness. Tall Mrs. Alexander always kept in the background so far as the renting of rooms was concerned, determined not to be confused with a landlady. Her hair was always glossy black, new from the hairdresser, her nails polished red. She stepped in and out of the house with a polite nod like another, but more superior, tenant. I fairly drank her in with my mind while smiling politely back. I had nothing whatsoever against these Alexanders except in the matter of their wanting me to take on a higher-priced room. If he had thrown me out I would still have had nothing much against them, I would mainly have been fascinated. In a sense I felt that the swine Alexander was quite excellent as such, surpassingly hand-picked. And although I wanted to avoid him on my return to my lodging I knew very well I had something to gain from a confrontation, should it happen. In fact, I was aware of a *daemon* inside me that rejoiced in seeing people as they were, and not only that, but more than ever as they were, and more, and more.

At that time I had a number of marvellous friends, full of good and evil. I was close on penniless but my spirits were all the more high because I had recently escaped from the Autobiographical Association (non-profit-making) where I was thought rather mad, if not evil. I will tell you about the Autobiographical Association.

Ten months before the day when I sat writing my poem on the worn-out graves of the dead in Kensington and had a conversation with the shy policeman, "Dear Fleur," came the letter.

"Dear Fleur." Fleur was the name hazardously bestowed at birth, as always in these cases before they know what you are going to turn out like. Not that I looked too bad, it was only that Fleur wasn't the right name, and yet it was mine as are the names of those melancholy Joys, those timid Victors, the inglorious Glorias and materialistic Angelas one is bound to meet in the course of a long life of change and infiltration; and I once met a Lancelot who, I assure you, had nothing to do with chivalry.

However all that may be, "Dear Fleur," went the letter. "I think I've found a job for you! . . ." The letter went on, very boring. It was a well-wishing friend and I have forgotten what she looked like. Why did I keep these letters? Why? They are all neatly bundled up in thin folders, tied with pink tape, 1949, 1950, 1951 and on and on. I was trained to be a secretary; maybe I felt that letters ought to be filed, and I'm sure I thought they would be interesting one day. In fact, they aren't very interesting in themselves. For example about this time, just before the turn of the half-century, a bookshop wrote to ask for their money or they would "take further steps." I owed money to bookshops in those days; some were more lenient than others. I remember at the time thinking the letter about the further steps quite funny and worth keeping. Perhaps I wrote and told them that I was quite terrified of their steps approaching further, nearer, nearer; perhaps I didn't actually write this but only considered doing so. Apparently I paid them in the end for the final receipt is there, £5.8.9. I always desired books; nearly all of my bills were for books. I possessed one very rare book which I traded for part of my bill with another bookshop, for I wasn't a bibliophile of any kind; rare books didn't interest me for their rarity, but for their content. I borrowed frequently from the public library, but often I would go into a book-shop and in my longing to possess, let us say, the Collected Poems of Arthur Hugh Clough and a new Collected Chaucer, I would get into con-versation with the bookseller and run up a bill.

"Dear Fleur, I think I've found a job for you!"

I wrote off to the address in Northumberland setting forth my merits as a secretary. Within a week I got on a bus to go and be interviewed by my new employer at the Berkeley Hotel. It was six in the evening. I had allowed for the rush hour and arrived early. He was earlier still, and when I went to the desk to ask for him he rose from a nearby chair and came over to me.

He was slight, nearly tall, with white hair, a thin face with high cheekbones which were pink-flushed, although otherwise his face was pale. His right shoulder seemed to protrude further than the left as if fixed in the position for shaking hands, so that his general look was very slightly askew. He had an air which said, I am distinguished. Name, Sir Quentin Oliver.

We sat at a table drinking dry sherry. He said, "Fleur Talbot—are you half French?"

"No. Fleur was just a name my mother fancied."

"Ah, interesting. . . . Well now, yes, let me explain about the undertaking."

The wages he offered were of 1936 vintage, and this was 1949, modern times. But I pushed up the starting price a little, and took the job for its promise of a totally new experience.

"Fleur Talbot . . ." he had said, sitting there in the Berkeley. "Any connection with the Talbots of Talbot Grange? The Honourable Martin Talbot, know who I mean?"

I said, "No."

"No relation to them. Of course there are the Talbots of Findlays Refineries. Those sugar people. She's a great friend of mine. Lovely creature. Too good for him if you ask my opinion."

Sir Quentin Oliver's London flat was in Hallam Street near Portland Place. There I went to my job

13

from nine in the morning till five-thirty in the afternoon, passing the B.B.C. edifice where I always hoped to get a job but never succeeded.

At Hallam Street every morning the door would be opened by Mrs. Tims, the housekeeper. The first morning Sir Quentin introduced her to me as "Beryl, Mrs. Tims," which she in a top-people's accent corrected to Mrs. Beryl Tims, and while I stood waiting with my coat on, they had an altercation over this, he maintaining politely that before her divorce she had been Mrs. Thomas Tims and now she was, to be precise, Beryl, Mrs. Tims, but in no circumstances was Mrs. Beryl Tims accepted usage. Mrs. Tims then announced she could produce her National Insurance card, her ration book and her identity card to prove that her name was Mrs. Beryl Tims. Sir Quentin held that the clerks employed in the ministries which issued these documents were ill-informed. Later, he said, he would show her what he meant under correct forms of address in one of his reference books. After that, he turned to me.

"I hope you're not argumentative," he said. "An argumentative woman is like water coming through the roof; it says so in the Holy Scriptures, either Proverbs or Ecclesiastes, I forget which. I hope you don't talk too much."

"I talk very little," I said, which was true, although I listened a lot because I had a novel, my first, in larva. I took off my coat and handed it somewhat snootily to the refined Mrs. Tims, who took it away roughly and stalked off hammering

14

the parquet floor with her heels. As she went she
looked contemptuously at the coat which was a
cheap type known then as "Utility." Utility was at
that time the people's garment, recognizable by
the label with its motif of overlapping quarter-
moons. Many of the rich, who could afford to
spend clothing coupons on non-Utility at Dor-
ville, Jacqmar or Savile Row, still chose to buy
Utility, bestowing upon it, I noticed, the inevita-
ble phrase, "perfectly all right." I have always
been on the listen-in for those sorts of phrases.

But perfectly all right was not what Beryl Tims
thought of my coat. I followed Sir Quentin into
the library. "Come into my parlour said the
spider to the fly," said Sir Quentin. I acknowledged his witticism with the smug smile which I
felt was part of my job.

In the interview at the Berkeley he had told me
the work was to be of a ". . . literary nature. We are
a group. A group, I may add, of some distinction.
Your function will be highly interesting, although
of course on you will depend the efficiency and
typewriting—how I hate that word stenography, so
American—and of course the stationery cupboard
is dreadfully untidy at the moment and will need
seeing to. You will have your work cut out, Miss
Talbot."

I had asked at the end of the interview if I could
get some pay at the end of the first week as I
couldn't hold out for a whole month. He went
aloof, a little hurt. Perhaps he suspected that I
wanted to put the job on a week's trial; this was

partly true, but my need for speedy pay was equally true. He had said, "Oh well, yes, of course if it's a case of *hardship*," as one might say a case of sea-sickness. In the meantime I had wondered why he had called the interview at a London hotel instead of at the flat where I was to work.

Now that I was actually in the flat he answered that question himself. "It isn't everybody, Miss Talbot, whom I invite to enter my home." I replied agreeably that we all felt like that and I cast my eyes round the room; I couldn't see the books, they were all behind glass. But Sir Quentin was not satisfied with my "We all feel like that"; it put us on an equal footing. He set about making plain that I had missed the point. "What I mean," he said, "is that here we have formed a very special circle, for a very delicate purpose. The work is top secret. I want you to remember that. I interviewed six young ladies, and I have chosen you, Miss Talbot, I want you to remember that." By this time he was seated at his very splendid desk, leaning back in his chair, eyes half-closed, with his hands held before him at chest level, the finger-tips of each hand touching the other. I sat at the opposite side of the desk.

He waved towards a large antique cabinet. "In there," he said, "are secrets."

I wasn't alarmed, for although he was plainly some sort of crank and it struck me, of course, that he might be up to no good, there was nothing in his voice or manner that I felt as an immediate personal menace. But I was on the alert, in fact excited. The novel I was writing, my first, *Warrender Chase,* was really filling my whole life at that time. I was finding it extraordinary how, throughout all the period I had been working on the novel, right from Chapter One, characters and situations, images and phrases that I absolutely needed for the book simply appeared as if from nowhere into my range of perception. I was a magnet for experiences that I needed. Not that I reproduced them photographically and literally. I didn't for a moment think of portraying Sir Quentin as he was. What gave me great happiness was his gift to me of the finger-tips of his hands touching each other, and, nestling among the words, as he waved towards the cabinet, "In there are secrets," the pulsating notion of how much he wanted to impress, how greatly he desired to believe in himself. And I might have left the job then and there, and never seen or thought of him again, but carried away with me these two items and more. I felt like the walnut cabinet itself towards which he was waving. In here are secrets, said my mind. At the same time I gave him my total attention.

After all these years I've got used to this process of artistic apprehension in the normal course of the day, but it was fairly new to me then. Mrs. Tims had also excited me in the same way. An awful woman. But to me, beautifully awful. I must say that in September of 1949 I had no idea at all if I could bring off *Warrender Chase*. But whether I was capable of finishing the whole book or not, the excitement was the same.

Sir Quentin went on to tell me what the job was about. Mrs. Tims brought in the post.

Sir Quentin ignored her but he said to me, "I never deal with my correspondence until after breakfast. It's too upsetting." (You must know that in those days the mail arrived at eight in the morning and people who didn't go out to work read their letters with their breakfast, and those who did, read them on the bus.) "Too upsetting." In the meantime Mrs. Tims went to the window and said, "They're dead." She was referring to a bowl of roses which had shed their petals on the table. She gathered up the petals and stuck them into the rose bowl, then lifted the rose bowl to carry it away. As she did so she looked at me and caught me watching her. I continued to watch the spot where she had been, as if in glaze-eyed abstraction, and perhaps, thus, I succeeded in fooling her that I hadn't been consciously watching her at all, only looking at the spot where she stood, my thoughts on something else; perhaps I didn't fool her, one never knows about those things. She continued to grumble about the dead roses till she left the room, looking all the more like the wife of a man I knew; Mrs. Tims even walked like her.

I turned my attention to Sir Quentin, who waited for his housekeeper's exit with his eyes half-shut, and his hands in an attitude almost of prayer, his

18

elbows on the arm-rests of his chair, his finger-tips touching.

"Human nature," said Sir Quentin, "is a quite extraordinary thing, I find it quite extraordinary. You know the old adage, truth is stranger than fiction?"

I said yes.

It was a dry sunny day of September 1949. I remember looking towards the window where intermittent sunlight fingered the muslin curtains. My ears have a good memory. If I recall certain encounters of the past at all, or am reminded perhaps by old letters that they happened, back come flooding the aural images first and the visual second. So I remember Sir Quentin's way of speech, his words precisely and his intonation as he said to me, "Miss Talbot are you interested in what I am saying?"

"Oh, yes. Yes, I agree that truth is stranger than fiction."

I had thought his eyes were too shut-in on his thoughts to notice my head turning towards the window. I know that I had looked away to register within myself some instinctive thoughts.

"I have a number of friends," he said, and waited for this to sink in. Dutifully now, I kept my eyes on his words.

"Very important friends, V.I.P.s. We form an association. Do you know anything about the British laws of libel? My dear Miss Talbot, these laws are very narrow and very severe. One may not, for instance, impugn a lady's honour, not that one would wish to were she in fact a lady, and as for stating the actual truth about one's life which naturally involves living people, well, it is quite impossible. Do you know what we have done, we who have lived extraordinary—and I mean extraordinary—lives? Do you know what we have done about placing the facts on record for posterity?"

I said no.

"We have formed an Autobiographical Association. We have all started to write our memoirs, the truth, the whole truth and nothing but the truth. And we are lodging them for seventy years in a safe place until all the living people mentioned therein shall be living no longer."

He pointed to the handsome cabinet faintly lit by the sun filtering through the gathered muslin curtains. I longed to be outside walking in the park and chewing over Sir Quentin's character in my mind before even finding out any more about him.

"Documents of that sort should go into a bank vault," I said.

"Good," said Sir Quentin in a bored way. "You are quite right. That is possibly the ultimate destination of our biographical reminiscences. But that is looking ahead. Now I have to tell you that my friends are largely unaccustomed to literary composition; I, who have a natural bent in that field, have taken on the direction of the endeavour. They are, of course, men and women of great distinction living full, very full, lives. One way and another these days of change and postwar. One can't expect. Well, the thing is I'm helping them to write their memoirs which they haven't time to do. We have friendly meetings, gatherings, get-togethers and so on. When we are better organized we shall meet at my property in Northumberland."

Those were his words and I enjoyed them. I thought them over as I walked home through the park. They had already become part of my memoirs.

At first I supposed Sir Quentin was making a fortune out of the memoir business. The Association, as he called it, then comprised ten people. He gave me a bulky list of the members' names with supporting biographical information so selective as to tell me, in fact, more about Sir Quentin than the people he described. I remember quite clearly my wonder and my joy at:

> Major-General Sir George C. Beverley, Bt. C.B.E., D.S.O., formerly in that "crack" regiment of the "Blues" and now a successful, a very successful business man in the City and on the Continent. General Sir George is a cousin of that fascinating, that infinitely fascinating hostess, Lady Bernice "Bucks" Gilbert, widow of the former chargé d'affaires in San Salvador, Sir Alfred Gilbert, K.C.M.G., C.B.E. (1919) whose portrait, executed by that famous, that illustrious, portrait painter Sir Ames Baldwin, K.B.E., hangs in the magnificent North Dining Room of Landers Place, Bedfordshire, one of the family prop-

erties of Sir Alfred's mother, the late incomparable Comtesse Marie-Louise Torri-Gil, friend of H.M. King Zog of Albania and of Mrs. Wilks, who as a debutante in St. Petersburg was a friend of Sir Q., the present writer, and daughter of a Captain of the Horse at the Court of the late Czar before her marriage to a British Officer, Lieutenant Wilks.

I thought it a kind of poem, and all in a moment I saw Sir Quentin, a good thirty-five years my senior as he was, in the light of a solemn infant intently constructing his wooden toy castle with its moats and turrets; and again, I thought of this piece of art, the presentation of Major-General Sir George C. Beverley and all his etceteras, under the aspect of an infinitesimal particle of crystal, say sulphur, enlarged sixty times and photographed in colour so that it looked like an elaborate butterfly or an exotic sea flower. From this first entry alone on Sir Quentin's list, I thought of numerous artistic analogies to his operations and I realized, all in that moment, how much religious energy he had put into it.

"You should study that list," Sir Quentin said.

The telephone rang and the door of the study was thrown open, both at the same time. Sir Quentin lifted the receiver and said "Hallo" while his eyes turned to the door in alarm. In tottered a tall, thin and extremely aged woman with a glittering appearance, largely conveyed by her many

22

strings of pearls on a black dress and her bright silver hair; her eyes were deeply sunk in their sockets and rather wild. Sir Quentin was meantime agitating into the phone: "Oh, Clotilde, my dear, what a pleasure—just one moment, Clotilde, I have a disturbance . . ." The old woman advanced, her face cracked with make-up, with a scarlet gash of a smile. "Who's this girl?" she said, meaning me.

Quentin had placed his hand over the receiver. "Please," he said in an anguished hush, fluttering his other hand, "I am talking on the telephone to the Baronne Clotilde du Loiret."

The old woman shrieked. I supposed she was laughing but it was difficult to tell. "I know who she is. You think I'm ga-ga, don't you?" She turned to me. "He thinks I'm ga-ga," she said. I noticed her fingernails, overgrown, so that they curled over the tips like talons; they were painted dark red. "I'm not ga-ga," she said.

"Mummy!" said old Sir Quentin.

"What a snob he is," screamed the mother.

Beryl Tims turned up just then and grimly promoted the old lady's withdrawal; Beryl glared at me as she left. Sir Quentin resumed his conversation on the phone with many apologies.

His snobbery was immense. But there was a sense in which he was far too democratic for the likes of me. He sincerely believed that talent, although not equally distributed by nature, could be later conferred by a title or acquired by inherited rank. As for the memoirs they could be

23

written, invented, by any number of ghost writers. I suspect he really believed that the Wedgwood cup from which he daintily sipped his tea derived its value from the fact that the social system had recognized the Wedgwood family, not from the china that they had exerted themselves to make.

By the end of the first week I had been let into the secrets of the locked cabinet in Sir Quentin's study. It held ten unfinished manuscripts, the products of the members of the Autobiographical Association.

"These works when completed," said Sir Quentin, "will be both valuable to the historian of the future and will set the Thames on fire. You should easily be able to rectify any lack or lapse in form, syntax, style, characterization, invention, local colour, description, dialogue, construction and other trivialities. You are to typewrite these documents under conditions of extreme secrecy, and if you succeed in giving satisfaction you may later sit in at some of our sessions and take notes."

His aged Mummy came and went from his study whenever she could slip away from Beryl Tims. I looked forward to her interruptions as she came waving her red talons and croaking that Sir Quentin was a snob.

At first I suspected strongly that Sir Quentin himself was a social fake. But as it turned out he was all he claimed to be by way of having been to Eton and Trinity College, Cambridge; he was a member of three clubs of which I only recall

White's and the Bath, he was moreover a baronet and his refreshing Mummy was the daughter of an earl. I was right but only in part, when I accounted to myself for his snobbery, that he had decided to make a profitable profession out of these facts themselves. And indeed it crossed my mind during that first week how easily he could turn his locked-up secrets to blackmail. It was much later that I found that this was precisely what he was doing; only it wasn't money he was interested in.

Going home at six o'clock in the golden dusk of that lovely autumn, I would walk to Oxford Street, take a bus to Speaker's Corner at Hyde Park, then cross the Park to Queen's Gate. I was fascinated by the strangeness of the job. I made no notes at all, but most nights I would work on my novel and the ideas of the day would reassemble themselves to form those two female characters which I created in *Warrender Chase,* Charlotte and Prudence. Not that Charlotte was entirely based on Beryl Tims, not by a long way. Nor was my ancient Prudence anything like a replica of Sir Quentin's Mummy. The process by which I created my characters was instinctive, the sum of my whole experience of others and of my own potential self; and so it always has been. Sometimes I don't actually meet a character I have created in a novel until some time after the novel has been written and published. And as for my character Warrender Chase himself, I already had him outlined and fixed, long before I saw Sir Quentin.

Now that I come to write this section of my

autobiography I remember vividly, in those days when I was writing *Warrender Chase,* without any great hope of ever getting it published, but with only the excited compulsion to write it, how I walked home across the park one evening, thinking hard about my novel and Beryl Tims as a type, and I stopped in the middle of the pathway. People passed me, both ways, going home from their daily work, like myself. Whatever I had been specifically thinking about the typology of Mrs. Tims went completely out of my mind. People passed me as I stood. Young men with dark suits and girls wearing hats and tailored-looking coats. The thought came to me in a most articulate way: "How wonderful it feels to be an artist and a woman in the twentieth century." That I was a woman and living in the twentieth century were plain facts. That I was an artist was a conviction so strong that I never thought of doubting it then or since; and so, as I stood on the pathway in Hyde Park in that September of 1949, there were as good as three facts converging quite miraculously upon myself and I went on my way rejoicing.

I thought often of Beryl Tims, a type of woman whom I had come to identify in my mind as the English Rose. Not that they resembled English roses, far from it; but they were English roses, I felt, in their own minds. The type sickened me and I was fascinated, such being the capacity of my imagination and my need to know the utmost. Her simpering when alone with me, her acquisitive greed, already fed my poetic vigilance to the extent that I simpered somewhat myself to egg her on and I think I even exercised my own greed for her reactions by provoking them: She had admired a brooch I wore; it was my best, a painted miniature on ivory, oval, set in a copper alloy. It was an eighteenth century brooch. The painting was the head of a young girl with her hair rustically free. Beryl Tims admired it where it sat on my lapel, for I was wearing a matching coat and skirt which was right in those days. I hated Beryl Tims as I sat having my morning coffee with her in the kitchen and she simpered about my lovely brooch. I hated her so much I took it off and gave it to her really to absolve my own hatred. But the glint in her eyes, the gasp of her big thick-lipped mouth, rewarded me. "Do you mean it?" she said.

"Yes, of course."

"Don't you like it?"

"Yes, I do."

"Then why are you giving it away?" she said with the nasty suspiciousness of one who perhaps had always been treated badly. She pinned the brooch on her dress. I thought that perhaps Mr. Tims had given her a rough time. I said, "You can have it, have it with pleasure," and meant it. I took my coffee cup to the sink and rinsed it under the tap. Beryl Tims followed me with hers. "I get lipstick on the rim of my cup," she said. "Men don't like to see lipstick on the rim of your cup and your glass, isn't that so? And yet they like you to wear lipstick. I always get admired for the colour of my lipstick. It's called English Rose."

27

She really was very like my lover's awful wife. Next thing she said, "Men like to see a bit of jewellery on a girl."

It was always a question of what men liked when we were alone together. The second week of my job she asked me if I was going to get married.

"No, I write poetry. I want to write. Marriage would interfere." I said this in a natural way and without previous calculation, but it probably sounded lofty, for she looked at me in a shocked sort of way and said, "But you could get married and have children, surely, and write poetry after the children had gone to bed." I smiled at this. I was not a pretty girl but I knew that I had a smile that transformed my face and, one way and another, I had made Beryl Tims furious.

That shocked look of hers reminded me very strongly of the look on the face of my lover's wife, Dottie, on another occasion. I must say that Dottie was a better educated woman than Beryl Tims, but the look was the same. She had confronted me with my affair with her husband, which I thought tiresome of her. I replied, "Yes, Dottie, I love him. I love him off and on, when he doesn't interfere with my poetry and so forth. In fact I've started a novel which requires a lot of poetic concentration because, you see, I conceive everything poetically. So perhaps it will be more off than on with Leslie."

Dottie was relieved that she wasn't in danger of losing her man, at the same time as she was horrified by what she called my unnatural attitude, which in fact was quite natural to me.

"Your head rules your heart," she said in her horror. I told her this was a stupid way of putting things. She knew this was true but in moments of crisis she fell back on banalities. She was a moralist and accused me then of spiritual pride. "Pride goes before a fall," said Dottie. In fact if I had pride it was vocational in nature; I couldn't help it, and I've never found it necessarily precedes falls. Dottie was a large woman with a sweet young face, plump breasts and hips, thick ankles. She was a Catholic, greatly addicted to the cult of the Virgin Mary about whose favours she fooled herself quite a bit, constantly betraying her quite good mind by simpering about Our Lady.

However, having said her say, Dottie left it at that. I saw a bottle of scent in her bathroom called "English Rose," and this both repelled me and gave me happy comfort as confirming a character forming in my own mind. I learned a lot in my life from Dottie, by her teaching me some precepts which I could usefully reject. She learned nothing of use from me.

But Beryl Tims was the better English Rose and the more frightful. And just then, I saw her more frequently than I did Dottie. But I didn't see Beryl Tims fully in action until some weeks later, at an informal gathering of the Autobiographical Association whose members' memoirs I had been typing and putting into recognizable English sentences. Up to then I had seen how Beryl treated Sir Quentin, always with a provocative tone which failed to provoke in the way that she wished; Beryl could not see why, but then she was stupid.

"Men like you to stand up to them," she said to me, "but Sir Quentin sometimes takes me up wrongly. And I've got his mother to watch over, haven't I?" She positively battled with Sir Quentin; obviously she was trying to arouse him sexually, to no avail. Only a high rank or a string of titles could bring an orgiastic quiver to his face and body. But he kept Beryl Tims in a state of hope. Also, I had watchfully noted Beryl with the ancient Lady Edwina, Sir Quentin's Mummy. Beryl was her prison warder and companion.

Chapter Two

The memoirs written by the members of the Autobiographical Association, although none had got beyond the first chapter, already had a number of factors in common. One of them was nostalgia, another was paranoia, a third was a transparent craving on the part of the authors to appear likeable. I think they probably lived out their lives on the principle that what they were, and did, and wanted, should above all look pretty. Typing out and making sense out of these compositions was an agony to my spirit until I hit on the method of making them expertly worse; and everyone concerned was delighted with the result.

A meeting of the ten members of the Association was called for three in the afternoon of Tuesday, October 4th, five weeks after I had started the job. So far I hadn't met any of them, for their last monthly meeting had been held on a Saturday.

That morning Beryl Tims made a scene when Sir Quentin said, "Mrs. Tims, I want you to keep Mummy under control this afternoon."

"Under control," said Beryl. "You might well say under control. How can I keep her ladyship under control and serve tea at the same time? How can I

31

check her fluxive precipitations?" This last phrase I had taught Beryl myself to while away a dull moment when she had been complaining of the old lady's having wet the floor. I had only half expected my version to catch on.

"She should be in a home," Beryl said to Sir Quentin. "She needs a private nurse," and so she wailed on. Sir Quentin looked troubled but impressed. "Fluxive precipitations," he said, with his eyes abstractly on the side wall, as if he were tasting a wine new to his experience, but which he was prepared to go more than half-way towards approving.

Now, by this time I had become rather fond of Lady Edwina, I think largely because she had taken an extraordinary liking to me. But also I enjoyed her dramatic entrances and her amazing statements. I could see she was more in charge of her senses than she let appear to her son or to Beryl, for sometimes when I had been alone with her in the flat she had rambled on in a quite natural tone of voice. And for some reason on these occasions alone with me she would sometimes totter off to the lavatory in time. So that I presumed her incontinence and wild behaviour with Sir Quentin and Beryl was due to her either fearing or loathing both of them, and that in any case they got on her nerves.

"I can't take responsibility for your mother this afternoon, not me," Beryl stated through her English Rose lips, that morning before the meeting.

"Oh, dear," said Sir Quentin. "Oh, dear."

In swayed Lady Edwina herself to add to the confusion. "Think I'm ga-ga, don't you?—Fleur, my dear, do you think I'm ga-ga?"

"Of course not," I said.

"They want to hush me up but I'm damned if they will hush me up," she said.

"Mummy!" said Sir Quentin.

"They want to give me sleeping pills to keep me quiet this afternoon. That's funny. Because I'm not going to take any sleeping pills. This is my flat, isn't it? I can do what I like in my own flat, can't I? I can receive or not receive according to my likes, is that not so?"

I assumed that the old woman was rich. She had rattled on to me one day how her son wanted her to do something to avoid death duties, hand over her property to him, but she hadn't much property and anyway she was damned if she was going to be Queen Lear. And I hadn't responded much to this line of talk, preferring to switch her over to a quite lucid and interesting speculation as to the possible nature and characteristics of the defunct Queen Lear herself. There was really nothing wrong with Lady Edwina except that her son and Beryl Tims got her down. As to her bizarre appearance, I liked it. I liked to see her shaking, withered hand with its talons pointing accusingly, I liked the four green-ish teeth through which she hissed and cackled. She cheered up my job with her wild eyes and her pre-war tea-gowns of black lace or draped, patterned silk always hung with glittering beads. Now, as she stood confronting Mrs. Tims and Sir Quentin with her rights I wondered about the history of it all. This must have been going on for years. Beryl Tims was looking in a frigid sort of way at the carpet beneath Lady Edwina's feet, no doubt waiting for another fluxive precipitation. Quentin sat with his head thrown back, his eyes shut and his hands touching at the finger-tips as in precious prayer.

I said, "Lady Edwina, if you'd like to take a rest this afternoon then afterwards you could come home to supper with me."

She accepted the bribe with alacrity. They all accepted the bribe, with a gabble and clack: Take her in a taxi, I'll be delighted to pay, we can book a taxi for six, no, it's not necessary to book, I'm delighted to accept, my dear Miss Talbot, what an excellent, what a very original idea. The taxi will, . . . We can come and fetch you home, Mummy, in a taxi. My dear Miss Talbot, how grateful we are. Now, Mummy, after lunch you will go and rest in your room.

Lady Edwina wavered out of the study to call up her hairdresser on the telephone, for she had a young apprentice girl who always came at her bidding to do her hair. I remember how Sir Quentin and Beryl Tims went on about being so very grateful; it didn't occur to them that I might actually want to spend an evening with my new and ravaged friend, an embarrassment to them but not to me. I thought of what there was for supper:

tinned herring roes on toast with instant coffee and milk, a perfect supper for Lady Edwina at her age and for me at mine. The tins of roes and the coffee were part of a small hoard I kept of precious rarities. Food was tightly rationed in those days.

By half-past two she had gone to bed for her rest, having first looked in to tell me she had decided to wear her dove grey with the beaded top if only to spite Mrs. Tims, who had advised her to put on an old skirt and jumper that would go better with my bed-sitter. I told her she was quite right, and to wrap up warm.

"I have my chinchilla," she said. "Tims has got her eye on my chinchilla but I've left it to the Cochin Mission to be sold for the poor. That will give Tims something to think about when I die. If she survives me. Ha! But you never know."

Only six out of the ten members called to the meeting could come.

It was a busy afternoon. I sat at my typewriter in a corner of the study while in straggled the six.

I had probably expected too much of them. For years I had been working up to my novel *Warrender Chase* and had become accustomed to first fixing a fictional presence in my mind's eye, then adding a history to it. In the case of Sir Quentin's guests the histories had been presented before the physical characters had appeared. As they trooped in, I could immediately sense an abject depression about them. Not only had I read Sir Quentin's fabulous lists of Who was Who among them, but I had also read the first chapters of their pathetic memoirs, and through typing them out and emphatically touching them up I think I had begun to consider them inventions of my own, based on the original inventions of Sir Quentin. Now these people whose qualities he had built up to be distinguished, even to the last rarity, came into the study that calm and sunny October afternoon with evident trepidation.

Sir Quentin dashed and flitted around the room arranging them in chairs and clucking, and occasionally introducing me to them. "Sir Eric—my new and I might say very reliable secretary Miss Talbot, no relation it appears to the distinguished branch of that family to which your dear wife belongs."

Sir Eric was a small, timid man. He shook hands all round in a furtive way. I supposed rightly that he was the Sir Eric Findlay, K.B.E., a sugar-refining merchant whose memoirs, like the others, had not yet got farther than Chapter One: Nursery Days. The main character was Nanny. I had livened it up by putting Nanny and the butler on the nursery rocking-horse together during the parents' absence, while little Eric was locked in the pantry to clean the silver.

Sir Quentin's method at this early stage was to send round advance copies of the complete set of typed and improved chapters to each of the ten members so that each of the six members present, and the four absent, had already seen their own and the others' typescripts. Sir Quentin had at first considered my additions to be rather extravagant, don't you think, my dear Miss Talbot, a bit too-*too?* After a good night's sleep he had evidently seen some merit in my arrangement, having worked out some of the possibilities to his own advantage for the future; he had said next morning, "Well, Miss Talbot, let's try your versions out on them. After all, we are living in modern times." I had gathered, even then, that he had plans for inducing me to write more compromising stuff into these memoirs, but I had no intention of writing anything beyond what cheered up the boring parts of the job for the time being and what could feed my imagination for my novel *Warrender Chase.* So that his purposes were quite different from mine, yet at the same time they coincided so far as he had his futile plans as to how he could use me, and I was working at top pace for him: photocopy machines were not current in those days.

At the meeting I gave close attention to the six members without ever actually studying them with my eyes. I always preferred what I saw out of the corners of my eyes, so to speak. Besides little Sir Eric Findlay, the people present were Lady Bernice Gilbert, nicknamed Bucks, the Baronne Clotilde du Loiret, a Mrs. Wilks, a Miss Maisie Young, and an unfrocked priest called Father Egbert Delaney whose memoirs obsessively made the point that he had lost his frock through a loss of faith, not morals.

Now Lady Bernice Gilbert swam in and at first dominated the party. "Bucks!" said Sir Quentin, embracing her. "Quentin," she declared hoarsely. She was about forty, much dressed up in new clothes which people who could afford it were buying a lot of, since clothes had come off the ration only a few months ago. Bucks was got up in an outfit called the New Look, a pill-box hat with an eye-veil, a leg-of-mutton-sleeved coat and long swinging skirt, all in black. She took a chair close to me, her physical presence very scented. She was the last person I would have attached to her first chapter. Her story, unlike some of the others, was by no means illiterate in so far as she knew how to string sentences together. The story opened with herself, alone in a church, at the age of twenty.

However, I was called, at that moment, to shake hands with Miss Maisie Young, a tall, attractive girl of about thirty who walked with a stick, one of her legs being encased in a contraption which looked as if it was part of her life, and not a passing affair of an accident. I took considerably to Maisie Young; indeed I wondered what she was doing in this already babbling chorus; and still more I was amazed that she belonged to the opening of the memoirs attached to her name, this being an unintelligible treatise on the Cosmos and how Being is Becoming.

"Maisie, my dear Maisie, can I put you here? Are you comfortable? My dear Clotilde! My very dear Father Egbert, are you all comfortable? Let me take your wrap, Clotilde. Mrs. Tims—where is Mrs. Tims?—Miss Talbot, perhaps you would be so kind, so very kind as to take la Baronne Clotilde's . . ."

The Baronne Clotilde, whose ermine cape I took to the door and passed over to the bubbling Mrs. Tims outside, had set her memoirs in a charming French château near Dijon where, however, everything conspired to do down the eighteen-year-old Baronne. While I had the time to think at all, I was momentarily puzzled by the fact that in the autobiography Clotilde had been eighteen in 1936, whereas now in 1949 she was well into her fifties. But on to Father Egbert, who wore a Prince of Wales check jacket and grey flannel trousers; his face resembled a snowman's with small black pebbles for eyes, nose and mouth; his autobiography had begun, "It is with some trepidation that I take up my pen." Now he was shaking hands with Mrs. Wilks, a stout, merry-looking lady in her mid-fifties, clad in pale purple with numerous veil-like scarves, and painted up considerably. Since she had been brought up at the court of the Czar of Russia her memoirs should have been interesting, but so far she had written only a very dull account about the extreme nastiness of her three sisters and the discomforts of the royal palace, where all four girls had to share a bedroom.

All of these people's writings, with the exception of Bernice Gilbert's, were more or less illiterate. I now waited, as they first chattered and exclaimed, to hear what they thought of my improvements.

Mrs. Tims came into the study on some busy mission and told me in passing that Lady Edwina was sleeping peacefully.

It was to me a glorious meeting. The first twenty minutes were taken up with introductions and exclamations of all sorts; Father Egbert and Sir Eric, who apparently knew the four missing members, spent some time discussing them. Then Sir Quentin said, "Ladies and Gentlemen may I have your attention, please," and everybody stopped talking except Maisie Young who decided to finish what she was saying to me about the universe. She sat with her crippled leg in its irons stuck out in front of her, which did indeed give her a sort of right to hold forth longer than anybody else. Her handbag had a soft strap handle; I noticed that she held this handle threaded through her fingers like a horse-rein; I wasn't surprised to learn, later on, that Maisie's paralysed leg was the result of a riding accident.

The rest of the room was hushed and Maisie's voice went on, qualmless and strong, to assert, "There are some universal phenomena about which it is not for us mortals to enquire." I took very little notice of this silly proposition as such, although the actual words sound on in my mind. She had been talking quite a lot of nonsense, largely to the effect that autobiographies ought to start with the ultimates of the Great Beyond and not fritter away their time on the actual particulars

40

of life. I was thoroughly against her ideas; however, I had taken a liking to Maisie herself, and I particularly liked the way in which she went on, in the room which had been called to silence, insisting that there were things in life not to be enquired into, at the same time as she had opened her own autobiography with precisely these enquiries. Contradictions in human character are one of its most consistent notes and so I felt Maisie had a substantial character. Since the story of my own life is just as much constituted of the secrets of my craft as it is of other events, I might as well remark here that to make a character ring true it needs must be in some way contradictory, somewhere a paradox. And I'd already seen that where the self-portraits of Sir Quentin's ten testifiers were going all wrong, where they sounded stiff and false, occurred at points where they strained themselves into a constancy and steadiness that they evidently wished to possess but didn't. And I had thrown in my own bits of invented patchwork to cheer things up rather than make each character coherent in itself.

Sir Quentin, who was always polite to his customers, sat smiling while Maisie finished her emphatic say: "There are some universal phenomena about which it is not for us mortals to enquire."

Beryl Tims then charged in on some practical but unnecessary mission. It seemed that as she was being overlooked as a woman she was determined to behave as a man. Naturally she succeeded in drawing everyone's attention to herself, with her clatter and thumping, I forget what about.

When she had gone Sir Quentin made to resume his introductory speech but he had to lay it aside. Sir Eric Findlay spoke. He had obviously summoned up courage to do so.

"I say, Quentin," he said, "my memoirs have been tampered with."

"Oh, dear," said Sir Quentin. "I hope they're none the worse for it. I can arrange to delete any offensive item."

"I didn't say offensive," said Sir Eric, looking nervously around the room. "Indeed, you have made some very interesting changes. Indeed, I wondered how you guessed that the butler locked me in the pantry to clean the silver, which he did indeed. Indeed he did. But Nanny on the rocking-horse, well, Nanny was a very religious woman. On my rocking-horse with our butler, indeed, you know. It isn't the sort of thing Nanny would have done."

"Are you sure?" said Sir Quentin, pointing a coy finger at him. "How can you be sure if you were locked in the pantry at the time? In your revised memoir you found out about their prank from a footman. But if in reality . . ."

"My rocking-horse was not at all a sizeable one," said Sir Eric Findlay, K.B.E., "and Nanny, though not plump, would hardly fit on it with the butler who was, though thin, quite strong."

"If I might voice an opinion," said Mrs. Wilks, "I

42

thought Sir Eric's piece very readable. It would be a pity to sacrifice the evil nanny and the dastardly butler having their rock on the small Sir Eric's horse, and I like particularly the stark realism of the smell of brilliantine on the footman's hair as he bends to tell the small Sir Eric-that-was of his discovery. It explains so much the Sir Eric-that-is. Psychology is a wonderful thing. It is in fact all."

"My nanny was not actually evil," murmured Sir Eric. "In fact—"

"Oh, she was utterly evil," Mrs. Wilks said.

"I quite agree," said Sir Quentin. "She was plainly a sinister person."

Lady Bernice "Bucks" Gilbert said in her bronchial voice, "I suggest you leave your memoir as Quentin has prepared it, Eric. One has to be objective about such things. I think it vastly superior to the opening chapter of my memoirs."

"I will sleep on it," said Eric mildly.

"And your memoir, Bucks?" Sir Quentin said anxiously. "Don't you care for it to date?"

"I do and I don't, Quentin. There's something missing."

"That can be remedied, my dear Bucks. What is missing?"

"A *je ne sais quoi*, Quentin."

"But," said the Baronne Clotilde du Loiret, "you know, Bucks, I thought your piece was very much you. My dear, the atmosphere as the curtain rises as it were. As the curtain rises on you in the empty church. In the empty church with the fragrance of

43

incense and you praying to the Madonna in your hour of need. I was carried away, Bucks. I mean it. Then comes Father Delaney and lays his hand on your shoulder—"

"I wasn't there. It wasn't I." This was Father Egbert Delaney speaking up. "There is a mistake here that needs rectifying." He looked at Sir Quentin and then at me with his round pebbly eyes and his pudgy hands clasped together. He looked from me back to Sir Quentin. "I must say in all verity that I am not the Father Delaney described in Lady Bernice's opening scene. Indeed I was a seminarian at the Beda in Rome at the time she refers to."

"My dear Father," said Sir Quentin, "we need not be too literal. There is such a thing as the economy of art. However, if you object to being named—"

"It was with some trepidation that I took up my pen," Father Delaney declared, and then he looked with horror at the women, including myself, and with terror at the men.

"I didn't actually name the priest," said Bucks. "I never said that all this exchange took place in the church, I only—"

"Oh but it has an effect of great *tendresse*," said Mrs. Wilks. "My memoir is nothing like as touching, would that it were. My memoir—"

But Lady Edwina just then came tottering into the room. "Mummy!" said Sir Quentin.

I jumped up and pulled forward a chair for her.

44

Everyone was jumping up to do something for her. Sir Quentin fluttered his hands, begged her to go and rest and demanded, "Where is Mrs. Tims?" He obviously expected his mother to make a scene, and so did I. However, Lady Edwina didn't make it. She took over the meeting as if it were a drawing-room tea party, holding up the proceedings with the blackmail of her very great age and of her newly revealed charm. I was greatly impressed by the performance. She knew some of them by name, enquired of their families so solicitously that it hardly mattered that most of them were long since dead, and when Mrs. Tims entered with the tea and soda buns on a tray, exclaimed, "Ah Tims! What delightful things have you brought us?" Beryl Tims was amazed to see her sitting there, wide awake, with her powdered face and her black satin tea-dress freshly spoiled at the neck and shoulders with a slight face-powder overflow. Mrs. Tims was furious but she put on her English Rose simper, and placed the tray with solicitude on the table beside old Edwina, who was at that moment enquiring of the unfrocked father, "Are you the Rector of Wandsworth in civilian clothing?"

"Lady Edwina, your rest hour," wheedled Mrs. Tims. "Come along, now. Come with me."

"Dear no, oh dear no," said Father Egbert, sitting up and putting to rights his Prince of Wales jacket. "I don't belong to a religious hierarchy of any persuasion!"

"Funny, I smell a clergyman off you," said Edwina.

"Mummy!" said Sir Quentin.

"Come now," said Mrs. Tims, "this is a serious meeting, a business meeting that Sir Quentin—"

"How do you take your tea?" said Lady Edwina to Maisie Young. "Weak? Strong?"

"Middling please," said Miss Young, and looked at me sideways from under her soft felt hat as if to gain courage.

"Mummy!" said Quentin.

"Whatever have you done to your leg?" said Lady Edwina to Maisie Young.

"An accident," replied Miss Young, softly.

"Lady Edwina! What a thing to ask . . ." said Mrs. Tims.

"Take your hand off my arm, Tims," said Edwina.

After she had poured tea, and asked the Baronne Clotilde how she had managed to preserve her ermine cape without the smell of camphor, and I had helped Sir Quentin to pass the teacups, Edwina said, "Well, I must take my nap." She gave Beryl Tims's hand a shove-away and allowed Sir Eric to help her to her feet. When she had gone, followed by Mrs. Tims, everyone exclaimed, How charming, How wonderful for her age, What a grand old lady. They were going on like this in between bites of their soda buns and accompanied by a little orchestra of teaspoons on china, when Lady Edwina opened the door again and put her

46

head round it. "I enjoyed the service very much, I always hate hymn-singing," she said, and retreated.

Beryl Tims minced in and collected the tea things, muttering to me as she passed, "She's gone back to bed. Calling me Tims like that, what a cheek."

I sat at my typist's desk in the corner and made notes while they talked about their memoirs till six o'clock, half an hour past my time to go home.

"When I come to my war experiences," said Sir Eric, "that will be the time, the climax."

"It was during the war that I lost my faith," declared Father Egbert. "For me, too, it was a moment of climax. I wrestled with my God, the whole of one entire night."

Mrs. Wilks remarked that it was not every woman who had witnessed the gross indelicacies of the Russian revolution and survived, as she had. "It gives one a quite different sense of humour," she explained, without explaining anything.

I had been taking notes, there at my corner table. I recall that the Baronne Clotilde turned to me before she left and said, "Have you got everything that is germane?"

Maisie Young, leaning on her stick and with a hand still twined round her bag-strap as if it were a horse-rein, said to me, "Where can I find the book Father Egbert Delaney has been telling me about? It's an autobiography."

She had been conversing privately with the priest, apart from the hubbub. I turned to Father

47

Delaney, my pencil poised on my notebook, for enlightenment. "The *Apologia pro Vita Sua,*" he said, "by John Henry Newman."

"Where can I get it?" said Miss Young.

I promised to get her a copy from the public library.

"If one is writing an autobiography one should model oneself on the best shouldn't one?" she said.

I assured her that the *Apologia* was among the best.

Father Egbert murmured to himself, but for us two to hear, "Alas."

It was a quarter past six before they had left. I went to fetch Lady Edwina to take her home to have supper with me.

"She's fast asleep," Beryl Tims said. "And in any case she broke her promise to us, why should you be bothered with her?" Sir Quentin stood listening. Beryl Tims appealed to him. "Why should we pay for a taxi and all the bother? She interrupted the meeting, after all."

"Oh, but everybody was delighted," I said.

Sir Quentin said, "But speaking personally I had a *mauvais quart d'heure;* one never knows with my poor mother what she may say or do. I decline responsibility. A *mauvais quart d'heure*—"

"Let her sleep on," said Beryl Tims.

As I left Sir Quentin said to me, "We have a gentleman's agreement, you and I, that none of the Association's proceedings will ever be discussed or revealed, don't we? They are highly confidential."

Not being a gentleman by any stretch of the sense I cheerfully agreed; I have always been impressed by Jesuitical casuistry. But at the time I was thinking only of the meeting itself; it filled me with joy.

It was after seven when I got home. My landlord, Mr. Alexander, lumbered downstairs to meet me as I let myself into the hall. "An elderly party's waiting for you. I let her into your room as she needed to sit down. I let her use the bathroom as she needed to go. She wet the bathroom floor."

There, in my room, I found Lady Edwina, wrapped in her long chinchilla cape; she sat in my wicker arm-chair between the orange box which contained my food supply and a bookcase. She was beaming with pride. "I got away," she said. "I foiled them completely. There wasn't a taxi any-where but I got a lift from an American. Your books—what a lot there are. Have you read them all?"

I wanted to telephone to Sir Quentin to tell him where his mother was. There was a phone in my room connected to a switchboard in the basement. I got no reply, which was not unusual, and I rattled to gain attention. The red-faced house-boy, under-paid and bad-tempered, who lived with his wife and children down in those regions, burst into the room shouting at me to stop rattling the phone. Apparently the switchboard was in process of repair and a man was working overtime on it. "The board's asunder," bellowed the boy. I liked the phrase and picked it out for myself from the wreckage of the moment, as was my wont.

"Lady Edwina," I said, "will they know where you are? I can't get through on the phone."

"They will never know I'm out," she said. "As far as they're concerned I've gone to bed with a sleeping pill, but I dropped the pill down the lavatory pan. Call me Edwina which I don't permit, mind you, of Beryl Tims."

I got out cups and saucers and plates and set about making an evening of it. I propped the old lady's feet on three volumes of the complete Oxford English Dictionary. She looked regal, she looked comfortable; she had no difficulty with her bladder and only asked to be taken to the lavatory once; she cackled with delight over her herring roes comparing them to caviar "which is the same thing only a different species of fish."

"Your studio is so like Paris," she said. "Artists I have known . . ." She mused, "Artists and writers, they have become successful, of course. And you, too . . ."

Now I hastened to assure her that this wasn't likely. It rather frightened me to think of myself in a successful light, it detracted in my mind from the quality of my already voluminous writings from among which eight poems only had been published in little reviews.

I looked out an unpublished poem by which I set great store even though it had been rejected eight times, returning to roost in my own stamped and addressed envelope among my punctual morning letters, over a period of a year. It was perhaps because of its outcast fate that I felt an attachment to it. The old lady's hands clutched her chinchilla with her long red fingernails dug into the silver-grey pelt. The poem was entitled "Metamorphosis."

> This is the pain that sea anemones bear
> in the fear of aberration but wilfully
> aspiring to respire in another,
> more difficult way, and turning
> flower into animal interminably.

As I was reading this first verse my boy-friend Leslie let himself in the door with the spare key I had given him. He was tall and stoopy with a lock of blond hair falling over one eye and a fresh young face. I was proud of him.

"How are you?" said Edwina when I introduced him. She had told me that since she was forgetful of names and faces she always greeted people with "How are you?" in case she had met them before.

"I'm fine, thanks," said Leslie without returning the question. Very often he irritated me in the extreme by small wants of courtesy. He was very much absorbed with numerous private anxieties which he was too self-centred to overcome now, when I was presenting him with this splendid apparition, Edwina, an ancient, wrinkled, painted spirit wrapped in luxurious furs.

Edwina enquired kindly, as he took off his coat and sat on the divan bed, "What is your profession, Sir?"

"I'm a critic," said Leslie.

I was suddenly disenchanted with Leslie. It was a feeling that came over me ever more frequently, leading to quarrels in the end. Leslie just sat there and let himself be interviewed, unable to forget himself and his own concerns, with his young face and good health contrasting with Edwina's dotty shrewdness, her scarlet nails, her bright avid eyes. I saw in the pocket of Leslie's coat the top of a bottle which he had evidently brought along for the two of us. I pulled it out: smuggled Algerian wine.

"You're a music critic?" Edwina asked Leslie.

"No, a literary critic." He turned to me. "As a matter of fact, that poem you were reading—what was that line, 'aspiring and respiring' . . ?"

I put down the bottle and took up my poem.

"They think I've got a screw loose," said Edwina. "But I haven't got a screw loose. Ha!"

"A very bad line," said Leslie.

I read it out: "Aspiring to respire in another . . ." It seemed to me Leslie was right but I said, "What's wrong with it?"

"Is that a bottle of something?" Edwina said.

Leslie said, "Too feeble. Bad-sounding."

I said, "Edwina, it's Algerian wine. I would love you to have some but I think it would be bad for you."

"Let me open it," said Leslie, finding the cork-screw in a proprietory way. He was ambivalent about my writings, in that he often liked what I wrote but disliked my thoughts of being a published writer. This caused me to reject most of his criticism. As for his being a literary critic, that was not an untrue claim for he reviewed books for a periodical called *Time and Tide* and for other little reviews, although for his daily job he was a lawyer's clerk.

Leslie uncorked the bottle while Edwina assured him she was equal to a sip of Algerian wine.

There was a knock on my door. It was the irate house-boy with Mr. Alexander, my landlord, at his back.

"Someone is ringing up on Mr. Alexander's private number, 'tis a great inconvenience," said the boy. Mr. Alexander himself said, "The house phone's out of order. I can let you take this call in our sitting-room as your friend says it's urgent. But please tell your friends not to intrude further." He went on like this as I followed him to his sitting-room where his wife with her bubble-cut black hair sat stretching her long legs.

It was Sir Quentin on the phone. "Mummy is not here," he said, "We—"

"She's here with me. I'll bring her home."

"Oh, we've been so anxious, my dear Miss Talbot. We had great difficulty getting hold of you. Mrs. Tims—"

"Please don't ring this number again," I said. "The people object." I hung up and started to apologize to the Alexanders: "You see, there's an elderly lady . . ." They were looking at me with icy dislike as if my very voice was an offence. I got back to my own room quickly, where I found Leslie and Edwina drinking happily together. Edwina's charm was beginning to work on Leslie. He was reading her my poem and attacking it line by line.

He agreed to take Edwina home. He went out to phone someone and to find a taxi which he brought back to the door.

"I'll go straight home afterwards," he said to me as she toddled out on his arm. "Got to have an early night."

"Me too," I said. "I've got a lot to think about."

Edwina said, "He's jealous of you, Fleur," although what she meant I was not sure.

Before she was put in the taxi she said, "Is that a real Degas you have in your room?"

"School of," I said.

Leslie laughed, very delighted. I saw them off and went back to my room. I remember looking at my painting of two women with red pompoms in their brown hard hats, driving a carriage; and I wondered how it could be thought a Degas. It was an English painting signed J. Hayllar 1863.

I started to clear up and get ready for bed, on the whole deeply satisfied with my day, when I heard a woman singing "Auld Lang Syne" down in the street below my window. Now this was the signal that a very few of my friends used so that I could let them in at night without incurring the complaints of the implacable management and staff. I opened the window and looked out. I was astonished to see the large bulk of Leslie's wife Dottie in the lamplight, for it was already getting on for midnight and she had never so far called on me so late, if only for the reason that she might find her husband there. I imagined some emergency had brought her. "What's the matter, Dottie?" I said. "Leslie's not here."

"I know. He phoned me that he's taking an old woman friend of yours home and then he has to go to some literary party in Soho that he can't get out of. Fleur, I want to see you."

I heard a window open above my head. I didn't look up. I knew it was one of the Alexanders about to make a fuss. I merely said, "I'll let you in, Dottie." The upstairs window closed. I went down and let Dottie in, her sweet face swaddled in scarves, smelling of her English Rose scent.

I poured some Algerian wine. She began to cry. "Leslie," she said, "is using us both as a cover. He has someone else."

"Who is it?"

"I don't know. But it's a young poet, a man, I know for sure," said Dottie. "The love that dares not speak its name."

"A homosexual affair," I said, daring to speak its name somewhat to Dottie's added distress.

"Aren't you surprised?" she said.

"Not much." I was wondering how he found the time for us all.

"I was flabbergasted," Dottie said, "and hurt. So deeply wounded. You don't know what I'm suffering. I'm starting a novena to Our Blessed Lady of Fatima. I didn't suffer so much when I knew you were his mistress, Fleur, because—"

I interrupted her to cavil at the word "mistress," which I pointed out had quite different connotations from those proper to my independent liaison with poor Leslie.

"Why do you say 'poor Leslie,' why 'poor'?"

"Because obviously he's in difficulties with his life. Can't cope."

"Well he calls you his mistress. It's his word."

"It's an affectation. Poor Leslie."

"What am I to do?" she said.

"You could leave him. You could stay with him."

"I can't decide. I'm suffering. I'm only human."

I had known that sooner or later she would say she was only human. I sensed that in a short while she would come round to accusing me of not being human. Suddenly I had an idea.

"You could write your autobiography," I said. "You could join the Autobiographical Association where the members write their true life stories and have them put away for seventy years so that no living person will be offended. You might find it a relief."

It was after two in the morning before I got to

56

bed. I remember how the doings of my day appeared again before me, rich with inexplicable life. I fell asleep with a strange sense of sadness and promise meeting and holding hands.

Chapter Three

While I recount what happened to me and what I did in 1949, it strikes me how much easier it is with characters in a novel than in real life. In a novel the author invents characters and arranges them in convenient order. Now that I come to write biographically I have to tell of whatever actually happened and whoever naturally turns up. The story of a life is a very informal party; there are no rules of precedence and hospitality, no invitations.

In a discourse on drama it was observed by someone famous that action is not merely fisticuffs, meaning of course that the dialogue and the sense are action, too. Similarly, the action of my life-story in 1949 included the work I was doing when I put my best brains into my *Warrender Chase* most nights and most of Saturdays. My *Warrender Chase* was action just as much as when I was arguing with Dottie over Leslie, persuading her not to get him with child, as she came round the next night to tell me she was determined to do. My *Warrender Chase,* shoved quickly out of sight when my visitors arrived, or, lest the daily woman should clean it up when I left home in the morning for my job, took up the sweetest part of my mind and the rarest part of my imagination; it was like being in love and better. All day long, when I was busy with the affairs of the Autobiographical Association, I had my unfinished novel personified almost as a secret companion and accomplice following me like a shadow wherever I went, whatever I did. I took no notes, except in my mind.

Now the story of *Warrender Chase* was in reality already formed and by no means influenced by the affairs of the Autobiographical Association. But the interesting thing was, it seemed rather the reverse to me at the time. At the time; but thinking it over now, how could that have been? And yet, it was so. In my febrile state of creativity I saw before my eyes how Sir Quentin was revealing himself chapter by chapter to be a type and consummation of Warrender Chase, my character. I could see that the members of the Autobiographical Association were about to become his victims, psychological Jack the Ripper as he was.

My Warrender Chase was of course already dead by the end of my first chapter, where the family, his nephew Roland and his mother Prudence, are waiting for the eminent ambassador-poet and moralist to arrive, and where the car accident in which the great man Warrender dies is announced. You remember, perhaps, that, before his death is actually established, at the point where Roland's wife, Marjorie, finds that his face is unrecognizable, she says, "Oh, he'll have to have operations, like wearing a mask for the rest of his life!" I intended this to come out as one of those inane helpless things people say at moments of hysteria and shock. But it does transpire that he dies and it does in fact transpire that the mask is off, not on, for the rest of his life. His life, that is, in the pages of my novel, after Prudence, against the wishes of the rest of the family, confides Warrender's letters and other documents to the American scholar, Proudie. In my novel the documents were already in Proudie's hands when I began to see the trend of Sir Quentin's mind.

As you know I had already suspected that Sir Quentin was engaged in some form of racket, with maybe an eye to blackmail. At the same time I didn't see where the blackmail came in. He was not losing money on the project; on the other hand he was apparently quite rich and the potential victims of the Association were more marked in character by their once-elevated social position than for that outstanding wealth which tempts the crude blackmailer. Some of them had actually fallen on hard times.

I noticed by the correspondence that the four members who had not shown up at the meeting were already trying to wriggle out of it, and I too had decided that as soon as my vague uneasiness and my suspicions about Sir Quentin's motives should crystallize into anything concrete I would simply leave.

The four retreating members were a pharmaceutical chemist in Bath who pleaded pressure of business, and the much-cherished and widely connected Major-General Sir George Beverley who wrote in to say his memory was sadly failing, he couldn't, alas, recall anything of the past at all; there was also a retired headmistress from Somerset who wrote first to explain that her activities at the Tennis Club unfortunately precluded her giving time to her memoirs as she had hoped, and then, when further coaxed by Sir Quentin, gave a further excuse that her arthritis prevented her from the constant use of her typewriter or from taking up her pen. The fourth member to withdraw was that friend of mine who had got me the interview for the job. Now that I was established in the job I supposed she thought better of revealing her life-story to Sir Quentin since it would go through my hands. She wrote and told him that her biography was so interesting that she was going to write it with a view to publication; she also wrote to me on the same lines, begging me to sneak out the preliminary pages she had already given to Sir Quentin and post them back to her. Which I did. And Sir Quentin, I think, knew I had done this, for although he looked for my friend Mary's three pages and failed to find them in their place, he didn't ask me if I had done anything with them. I was quite ready to tell him I'd sent them back, but he merely looked at me with a smile and said, "Ah, well—interesting, were they not?"

"I don't know," I said. "I never read them." Which was true.

After some further cajoling letters from Sir Quentin to the four defectors, and ever more determined and, in a way, frightened replies from them, they got out of it. The chemist in Bath actually went so far as to get his solicitor to write to Sir Quentin firmly withdrawing from the Association. I sensed hysteria in the action of going to a solicitor when in fact the mere ignoring of Sir Quentin's letters would have had the same effect.

Well, what I found common to the members of Sir Quentin's remaining group was their weakness of character. To my mind this is no more to be despised than is physical weakness. We are not all born heroes and athletes. At the same time it is elementary wisdom always to fear weaknesses, including one's own; the reactions of the weak, when touched off, can be horrible and sudden. All of which is to say that I thought Sir Quentin was up to something quite dangerous in his evident attempt to get that group of weak people under his dominion for some purpose I couldn't yet make out. However, I confided all this to Dottie before I brought her in to the Autobiographical Association. I warned her not on any account to give herself away but to get some amusement if she could out of the proceedings. For I wanted some joy to enliven and transfigure those meetings and those writings, the solemn intensity of which was so vastly out of proportion to the subject-matter. However sinister the theme of my *Warrender Chase* which was then uppermost in my mind, no one can say it isn't a spirited novel. I think that ordinary readers would be astonished to know what troubles fell on my head because of the sinister side, and that is part of this story of mine; and that's what I think makes it worth the telling.

Dottie immediately set about making friends at the Autobiographical Association. She easily entered into the spirit of nostalgia; she felt herself persecuted and she had a great longing to be loved. I was alarmed at her sincerity and inability to detach herself from the situations of the others. I warned her, I kept on warning her that I suspected Sir Quentin was up to no good. Dottie said, "Have you planted me in that group for your own ends?"

"Yes. And I thought it might amuse you. Don't get dragged into it. Those people are infantile, and every day becoming more so."

"I shall pray for you," said Dottie, "to Our Lady of Fatima."

"Your Lady of Fatima," I said. Because, although I was a believer, I felt very strongly that Dottie's concept of religion was of necessity different from mine, in the same way that, years later when she made dramatic announcements that she had lost her faith I was rather relieved since I had always uneasily felt that if her faith was true then mine was false.

But now in my room after returning with me after a meeting at Sir Quentin's, Dottie said, "You planted me. I'll pray for you."

"Pray for the members of the Autobiographical Association," I said.

I don't know why I thought of Dottie as my friend but I did. I believe she thought the same way about me although she really didn't like me. In those days, among the people I mixed with, one had friends almost by predestination. There they were, like your winter coat and your meagre luggage. You didn't think of discarding them just because you didn't altogether like them. Life on the intellectual fringe in 1949 was a universe by itself. It was something like life in Eastern Europe to-day.

We were sitting talking over the meeting. It was already late November. I had argued with Dottie all the way home, on the bus and standing with her in a queue at a food-shop which ran out of stock of whatever it was Dottie had her eye on while the queue was still forming, and we the tenth; and anyway, it was closing time so that the brown-aproned grocer shut his doors with a click of the bolt and we plodded away.

The Autobiographical Association had taken her mind off Leslie. Neither of us had seen him for over three weeks. I had decided to finish with him as a lover, which was easy for me although I missed his face and his talk. Dottie was infuriated by my indifference, she desired so much that I should be in love with Leslie and not have him, and she felt I was cheapening her goods.

That afternoon was the third time I had attended a meeting of Quentin's autobiographers since I had been at the job. So far Dottie had produced no biographical writing of her own for the others to see. She had in fact written a long confessional piece about Leslie and his young poet and her consequent sufferings. I had torn it up, violently warning her against making any such true revelation. "Why?" said Dottie.

I couldn't tell her why. I didn't know why. I said I would be able to explain when I had written a few more chapters of my novel *Warrender Chase*.

"What has that got to do with it?" Dottie reasonably said.

"It's the only way I can come to a conclusion about what's going on at Sir Quentin's. I have to work it out through my own creativity. You have to follow my instinct, Dottie. I warned you not to give yourself away."

"But I like those people and Beryl Tims is so sweet. Sir Quentin's odd, but he's very reassuring, isn't he? Like a priest I once knew as a girl when I was at school with the nuns. And I'm sorry for him with that dreadful old mother. He has real goodness. . . ."

I sat with Dottie in my room trying to muddle my way into clarity. Whereas Dottie, with perfect clarity, was arguing a case for her own complete involvement, and I sensed trouble, either for her or from her.

"If you feel as you do," Dottie said, "you should leave the job."

"But I'm involved. I have to know what's going on. I sense a racket."

"But you don't want me to be involved," she said.

"No, it's dangerous. I wouldn't myself dream of getting involved with—"

"First you say you're involved. Next you say you

wouldn't dream of getting involved. The truth is," said Dottie, "that you resent me getting on so well with everybody, Sir Quentin and the members and Beryl."

She did get on well with everybody. That afternoon all of the remaining members had turned up, including Dottie, seven in all.

Mrs. Tims had immediately cornered Dottie to enquire in low tone, there in the entrance hall, if she had heard from her husband. Dottie murmured something with a soulful look. I was busy with the arrival of Maisie Young sportily managing with her bad leg, and nervous Father Egbert Delaney, but I had heard Beryl Tims exclaim from time to time in the course of Dottie's confidences, phrases such as "The swine!", "It's an abomination. They ought to be put on an island." I tried to get Dottie out of this but she was in no mind to follow me into the study until she had finished her chat with Beryl Tims. I had to abandon the two English Roses and be about my business.

During the past seven weeks the members who had remained faithful to the Association had seen some alarming changes made to their biographies. There was a certain day, late in October, when Sir Quentin told me, "I think your amusing elaborations of our friends' histories have so far been perfectly adequate, Miss Talbot, but the time has come for me to take over. I see that I must. It's a moral question."

I didn't object, but I had always found that people who said "It's a moral question" in that precise, pursed way that Sir Quentin said it were out to justify themselves, and were generally up to no good. "You see," said Sir Quentin, "they are being very frank, most of them, very frank indeed, but they have no sense of guilt. In my opinion . . ."

I had stopped listening. It was only a job. In many ways I was glad to be rid of the task of applying my inventiveness to livening up these dreary biographies. With the exception of Maisie Young who was still producing a quantity of material about the Beyond and the Oneness of life, they had started drafting out their first amorous adventures, egged on by Sir Quentin. I wouldn't have called them frank, as Sir Quentin rather too often did. All that had been achieved so far was Mrs. Wilks having had her blouse ripped open by a soldier before her escape from Russia in 1917; Baronne Clotilde had been caught in bed with her music tutor in the charming French château near Dijon; Father Egbert Delaney, he who had taken up his pen with some trepidation, had continued with the same trepidation for many pages to delineate the experience of impure thoughts the first time he had heard a confession; Lady Bernice "Bucks" Gilbert had effected a flashback to her teens, devoting a long chapter to her lesbian adventure with the captain of the hockey team, to which many descriptions of sunsets in the Cotswold hills lent atmosphere. With timid Sir Eric, it was a prep-school affair with another boy, the only interesting part of this adventure being that, while doing whatever he had unspecifically done with the other boy, young Eric's mind had dwelt all the time on an actress who had come to stay with his parents the last half-term.

Sir Quentin called these offerings "frank," with a most definite emphasis, and it bored me. "It's time for me to take over. It's a moral question," he said.

"I wish you hadn't torn up my piece," Dottie said as she sat with me in my room that late November evening. "It made me feel awful having nothing to offer."

"You seemed to have offered the whole story to Beryl Tims," I said.

"One has to confide in someone. She's a real friend. I think it's a scandal the way she has to run around after that revolting old woman."

In the past few weeks a nurse had been employed to take care of Lady Edwina. This nurse was a quiet woman, much despised by Beryl Tims. Certainly, Edwina was now no burden on Mrs. Tims and the old lady was wilder and funnier than ever. I really loved her. At the latest meeting of the Autobiographical Association, which I was now chewing over with Dottie, Edwina had made her appearance with the tea, dressed in pale grey velvet with long and many strings of pearls. Her rouged wrinkles and smudgy mascara were wonderful to behold. She had behaved with expressive graciousness and was continent; only when it was time to withdraw and the nurse tiptoed bashfully into the room to fetch her, Edwina had given vent to one of her long cackles followed by, "Well my dears, he's got you where he wants you, hasn't he? Ha! Trust my son Quentin." The bony index finger of her right hand pointed to Maisie Young. "Except you. He hasn't started on you, yet." Maisie's eyes were hypnotized by the long red fingernail pointed at her.

"Mummy!" said Quentin.

I had looked over to Dottie. She was murmuring with Beryl Tims, nodding wisely, very sympathetically.

I didn't reply to Dottie when, sitting sulkily that night in my room, she continued to emphasize how sorry she felt for Beryl Tims and how strongly she felt that Edwina should be sent to a home. It seemed to me Dottie was trying to provoke me. I could see Dottie was tired. For some reason I seldom remember feeling tired, myself, in those days; I suppose I must have felt exhausted at times for I got through an amazing variety and number of things in the course of every day; but I simply can't recall any occasion of weariness such as I could see in Dottie at that moment.

I made tea and I offered to read her a bit of my *Warrender Chase*. I did this for my own sake as much as to entertain, and, in a way, flatter her; for my own sake, though, because I intended to write some more pages of the book after Dottie went home, and this reading it over was a sort of preparation.

Now I had come to the bit where Warrender's nephew Roland and his wife Marjorie have decided to start going over Warrender's papers in

70

preparation for Proudie, for Prudence, Warrender's ancient mother, has appointed the scholar
Proudie to deal with them. This is three weeks
after the quiet country funeral for the family,
which I described in detail. Dottie had already
heard the funeral bit which she said was "far too
cold," but that hadn't bothered me; in fact I felt
her criticism was a rather good sign. "You haven't
brought home the tragedy of Warrender's death,"
Dottie had said. Which hadn't bothered me, either.
Anyway, this was the new chapter which is written
from Roland's point of view. Which was that his
uncle, Warrender Chase, had been a great man
tragically cut off in his prime; it has been abundantly acknowledged, it is a public commonplace.
He has successfully established his importance.

The family, secretly enjoying their stricken sta-
tus, are counting on Roland and Marjorie to do
their job conscientiously, to go through his papers
with Proudie and eventually produce a *Life and
Letters* or a memorial of some sort for Warrender
Chase; whatever they do, even if it takes years,
can't help but be interesting. The task naturally
saddens Roland, who leafs through the dead man's
papers. Warrender Chase, so vital a few weeks ago,
and now so absolutely gone. Roland is sad, a bit
unnerved. Why then has Marjorie, hitherto a
rather neurotic and droopy woman of thirty, begun to perk up? Her new bloom and spirits have
been increasingly noticeable day by day since the
funeral. Proudie is very well aware of Marjorie's
new happiness.

71

The above is of course a rough reminder. But when I read it to Dottie that evening in my bed-sitting-room I could see she wasn't liking it. I will quote the actual bit she finally objected to:

> "Marjorie," said Roland, "is there anything the matter with you?"
>
> "No, nothing at all."
>
> "That's what I thought," he said.
>
> "You seem to accuse me," she said, "of being all right."
>
> "Well I do, in a way. Warrender's death doesn't seem to have affected you."
>
> "It's affected her beautifully," said Proudie.

(I changed "beautifully" to "very well" before sending the book to the publisher. I had probably been reading too much Henry James at that time, and "beautifully" was much too much.)

It was at this point Dottie said, "I don't know what you're getting at. Is Warrender Chase a hero or is he not?"

"He is," I said.

"Then Marjorie is evil."

"How can you say that? Marjorie is fiction, she doesn't exist."

"Marjorie is a personification of evil."

"What is a personification?" I said. "Marjorie is only words."

"Readers like to know where they stand," Dottie said. "And in this novel they don't. Marjorie seems to be dancing on Warrender's grave."

Dottie was no fool. I knew I wasn't helping the reader to know whose side they were supposed to be on. I simply felt compelled to go on with my story without indicating what the reader should think. At the same time Dottie had given me the idea for that scene, towards the end of the book, where Marjorie dances on Warrender's grave.

"You know," Dottie said, "there's something a bit harsh about you, Fleur. You're not really womanly, are you?"

I was really annoyed by this. To show her I was a woman I tore up the pages of my novel and stuffed them into the wastepaper basket, burst out crying and threw her out, roughly and noisily, so that Mr. Alexander looked over the banisters and complained. "Get out," I yelled at Dottie. "You and your husband between you have ruined my literary work."

After that I went to bed. Flooded with peace, I fell asleep.

Next morning, after I had fished my torn pages of *Warrender Chase* out of the wastepaper basket and glued them together again, I went off to work, stopping on the way at the Kensington Public Library to get a copy of John Henry Newman's *Apologia*, which I had long promised to Maisie Young. She could quite well have procured it for herself during all those weeks, disabled though she was, but she belonged to that category of society, by no means always the least educated, who are always asking how they can get hold of a book; they know very well that one buys shoes from a shoe-shop and groceries from the grocer's, but to find and enter a bookshop is not somehow within the range of their imagination.

However, I felt kindly towards Maisie and I thought the sublime pages of Newman's auto-biography would tether her mind to the sweet world of living people, in a spiritual context though it was. Maisie needed tethering.

I found the book on the library shelves and while I was there in that section, I lit on another book I hadn't seen for years. It was the *Autobiography* of Benvenuto Cellini. It was like meeting an old friend. I borrowed both books and went on my way rejoicing.

Chapter Four

I began to take Edwina out for Sunday afternoons towards the end of November. It solved the problem of what to do with her when the nurse wasn't on duty and Mrs. Tims was off to the country with Sir Quentin. It suited me quite well because in the first place I liked her and secondly she fitted in so easily with my life. If the weather was fine I would fetch her in a taxi and then set her up in her folding wheel-chair for a walk along the edges of Hampstead Heath with a friend of mine, my dear Solly Mendelsohn, and afterwards we would go to a tea-shop or to his flat for tea. Solly was a journalist on a newspaper, always on night duty, so that I rarely saw him except in daylight hours.

There was nothing one couldn't discuss in front of Edwina; she was delighted with all we did and said, which was just as well, because Solly in his hours of confiding relaxation liked to curse and swear about certain aspects of life, although he had the sweetest of natures, the most generous possible heart. At first, in deference to the very aged Lady Edwina, Solly was cautious but he soon sized her up. "You're a sport, Edwina," he said.

Solly had a limp which he had won during the war; our progress was slow and we stopped in our tracks frequently, when the need to rest from our push-chair efforts somehow neatly combined with a point in our conversation that needed the emphasis of a physical pause, as when I told him that Dottie continued to complain about my *Warrender Chase* and consequently I was sorry I had ever started reading it to her.

"You want your brains examined," said Solly, limping along. He was a man of huge bulk with a great Semitic head, a sculptor's joy. He stopped to say, "You want your head examined to take notice of that silly bitch." Then he took his part of Edwina's pram-handle, and off we trundled again.

I said, "Dottie's sort of the general reader in my mind."

"Fuck the general reader," Solly said, "because in fact the general reader doesn't exist."

"That's what I say," Edwina yelled. "Just fuck the general reader. No such person."

I like to be lucid. So long as Dottie took in what I wrote I didn't care whether she disapproved or not. She would pronounce all the English Rose verdicts, and we often had rows, but of course she was a friend and always came back to hear more. I had been reading my book to Edwina and to Solly as well. "I remember," said Edwina in her cackling voice, "how I laughed and laughed over that scene of the memorial service for Warrender Chase that the Worshipful Company of Fishmongers put on for him."

Several people turned round to look at Edwina as she spoke with her high cry. People often turned round to stare at her painted wizened face, her green teeth, the raised, blood-red fingernail accompanied by her shrieking voice, the whole wrapped up to the neck in luxurious fur. Edwina was over ninety and might die any time, as she did about six years later. My dear, dear Solly lived into the seventies of this century, when I was far away. He started during his last illness to send me some of the books from his library that he knew I would especially like.

One of these books, which took me back over the years to wintry Hampstead Heath, was a rare edition of John Henry Newman's *Apologia pro Vita Sua* and another was a green-and-gold-bound edition, in Italian, of my beloved Benvenuto Cellini's *La Vita*.

Questa mia Vita travagliata io scrivo . . .

I remember Solly at his sweetest during those walks at Hampstead, with our Edwina always ready to support the general drama of our lives, crowing like a Greek chorus as we discussed this and that. I had not yet finished *Warrender Chase*, but Solly had found for me a somewhat run-down publisher with headquarters in a warehouse at Wapping who on the strength of the first two chapters was prepared to contract for it, on a down payment to me of ten pounds. I recall discussing the contract with Solly on one of our walks. It was a dry, windy day. We stopped while Solly scrutinised the one-page document. It fluttered in his hand. He gave it back to me. "Tell him to wipe his arse with it," said Solly. "Don't sign." "Yes, oh yes, oh yes!" screamed Edwina. "Just tell that publisher to wipe his arse with that contract."

I wasn't at all attracted to obscenities, but the combination of circumstances, something about the Heath, the weather, the wheel-chair, and also Solly and Edwina themselves in their own essence, made all this sound to me very poetic, it made me very happy. We wheeled Edwina into a tea-shop where she poured tea and conversed in a most polite and grand manner.

This, about the middle of December 1949. I had sat up many nights working on *Warrender Chase* and already had a theme for another novel at the back of my mind. I was longing to have enough money to be able to leave my job but until I could get enough money from a publisher there was no possibility of that.

And here comes a further point. My job at Sir Quentin's held my curiosity. What went on there could very well have continued to influence my *Warrender Chase* but it didn't. Rather, it was not until I had finished writing the book in January 1950 that I got some light on what Sir Quentin was up to.

It was the end of January 1950 that I began to notice a deterioration in all the members of the Association.

I had been down with 'flu and away from work

for two weeks. Just after the New Year Dottie had fallen ill with 'flu and I had spent most of my evenings with her in her flat, feeling fatalistically that I would catch her 'flu. I'm not sure that I didn't want to. During those first weeks of January when I went to Dottie's every night with the bits of shopping and things that she needed, Leslie often came round. He was no longer living with Dottie, having moved in with his poet. But something about the 'flu made Dottie very much more relaxed. She was less of the English Rose. She refrained from telling Leslie that she was praying for him. It is true she had some relics of her childhood, a teddy-bear, some dolls and a gollywog in bed with her, all lying along Leslie's side of the bed. She had always draped these toys on top of her bed, along the counterpane. I knew that they had got on Leslie's nerves but now that she was ill I suppose he felt indulgent, for he sometimes brought her flowers. There were no recriminations between us and we merrily skated on thick ice, while I privately wondered what I had ever seen in Leslie, he seemed so to have lost his good looks, at least in a virile sense. However, we were happy. Dottie even managed to laugh at some of my stories about Sir Quentin although at heart she was taking that Autobiographical Association very seriously.

Now that it was my turn to be ill I lay in bed all day with my high temperature, writing and writing my *Warrender Chase*. This 'flu was a wonderful opportunity to get the book finished. I worked till my hand was tired and until Dottie showed up at six in the evening with a vacuum flask of soup or some rashers of bacon which she fried on my gas ring, cutting them up kindly into little bits for me to swallow for my health's sake. She had got thinner from her own 'flu, and wisps of her hair fell down from its handsome upward twist so that she looked less English Rose for the time being. She had been to Sir Quentin's to give a helping hand in my absence.

"Dottie," I said, "you simply mustn't take that man seriously."

"Beryl Tims is in love with him," she said.

"Oh, God," I said.

I had just that day been writing the chapter in my *Warrender Chase* where the letters of my character Charlotte prove that she was so far gone in love with him that she was willing to pervert her own sound instincts, or rather forget that she had those instincts, in order to win Warrender's approval and retain a little of his attention. My character Charlotte, my fictional English Rose, was later considered to be one of my more shocking portrayals. What did I care? I conceived her in those feverish days and nights of my bout of 'flu, which touched on pleurisy, and I never regretted the creation of Charlotte. I wasn't writing poetry and prose so that the reader would think me a nice person, but in order that my sets of words should convey ideas of truth and wonder, as indeed they did to myself as I was composing them. I see no reason to keep silent about my enjoyment of the sound of my own voice as I work. I am sparing no relevant facts.

Now I treated the story of Warrender Chase with a light and heartless hand, as is my way when I have to give a perfectly serious account of things. No matter what is described it seems to me a sort of hypocrisy for a writer to pretend to be undergoing tragic experiences when obviously one is sitting in relative comfort with a pen and paper or before a typewriter. I enjoyed myself with Warrender's mother, Prudence, and her sepulchral sayings; and I made her hand over the documents to the American scholar Proudie whom she thought so comical. I did it scene by scene: Marjorie's obvious release from some terrible anxiety after Warrender's death and the consequent disapproval of her husband, Roland, with his little round face and his adoration of his dead uncle; then came the discovery of those letters and those notes left by Warrender Chase, pieced together throughout the book, which finally show with certainty what I had prepared the reader slowly to suspect. Warrender Chase was privately a sado-puritan who for a kind of hobby had gathered together a group of people specially selected for their weakness and folly, and in whom he carefully planted and nourished a sense of terrible and unreal guilt. As I wrote in the book, "Warrender's private prayer-meetings were of course known about, but only to the extent that they were considered too delicate a matter to be publicly discussed. Warrender had cultivated such a lofty myth of himself that nobody could pry into his life for fear of appearing vulgar." Well, he was supposed to be a mystic, known to be a pillar of the High Church of England; he made speeches at the universities, wrote letters to *The Times*. God knows where I got Warrender Chase from; he was based on no one that I knew.

I know only that the night I started writing *Warrender Chase* I had been alone at a table in a restaurant near Kensington High Street underground eating my supper. I rarely ate out alone, but I must have found myself in funds that day. I was going about my proper business, eating my supper while listening in to the conversation at the next table. One of them said, "There we were all gathered in the living-room, waiting for him."

It was all I needed. That was the start of *Warrender Chase,* the first chapter. All the rest sprang from that phrase.

But I invented for my Warrender a war record, a distinguished one, in Burma, and managed to make it really credible even though I filled in the war bit with a very few strokes, knowing, in fact, so little about the war in Burma. It astonished me later to find how the readers found Warrender's war record so convincing and full when I had said so little—one real war veteran of Burma wrote to say how realistic he found it—but since then I've come to learn for myself how little one needs, in the art of writing, to convey the lot, and how a lot of words, on the other hand, can convey so little.

I never described, in my book, what Warrender's motives were. I simply showed the effect of his

words, his hints. The real dichotomy in his character was in his public, formal High Churchism, and
his private sectarian style. In the prayer-meetings
he was a Biblical fundamentalist, to the effect, for
instance, that he induced one of his sect to give up
his good job in the War Office (as the Ministry of
Defence was then called), to sell all his goods to
feed the poor, and finally to die on a park bench
one smoggy November night. This was greatly to
Warrender's satisfaction. But he himself, I made
quite clear, understood Christianity in a far more
evolved and practical light. "Induced" is perhaps
not the word. He goaded with the Word of God
and terrorized. I showed how four women among
his prayer-set were his greatest victims, for he was a
deep woman-hater. One woman committed suicide, unable to stand the impressions of her own
guilt that he made upon her and convinced that
she had no friends; two others went mad, and this
included his housekeeper Charlotte, that English
Rose who was enthralled by him. His nephew's
wife, Marjorie, was on the point of mental crash
when the car crash killed Warrender. All these
years since, the critics have been asking whether
Warrender was in love with his nephew. How do I
know? Warrender Chase never existed, he is only
some hundreds of words, some punctuation, sentences, paragraphs, marks on the page. If I had
conceived Warrender Chase's motives as a psychological study I would have said so. But I didn't go
in for motives, I never have.

I covered the pages, propping them on the

underside of a tray, to finish *Warrender Chase* on my sick-bed that winter, even when my 'flu had turned bronchial and touched on pleurisy. I was too hoarse to read it to Dottie when she came to see me. But when she spoke of Sir Quentin and said, "Beryl Tims is in love with him," I sat up in my fever and said, "Oh, God!" The idea that anyone could be in love with Quentin Oliver was beyond me.

Chapter Five

I noticed the deterioration in the members of the Autobiographical Association precisely at the end of January 1950, a week after I had finished the book. I felt low from my 'flu but cheerful that my work was finished and behind me. I had no great hopes of success with *Warrender Chase* but already I had plans for a better book. Solly had found me another publisher to replace the one whose contract he had so despised. This publisher, an elderly man, was called Revisson Doe. He had a round, bald head of the shiny type I always wanted to stroke if I sat behind it in church or at the theatre. He said he thought *Warrender Chase* "quite evil, especially in its moments of levity," and that "the young these days are spiritually sick," but he supposed his firm could carry it at a loss in the hope of better books to come. He gave me what he said was the usual form of contract, on a printed sheet, and it wasn't such a bad contract nor was it a good one. Only, I found later by personal espionage that his firm, Park and Revisson Doe, had a private printing press on which they produced "the usual form of contract" to suit whatever they could get away with for each individual author. But

Revisson Doe commended himself to me by his entertaining reminiscences of his youth, when he was an office-boy on a literary weekly and had been sent out to Holborn Underground to meet W. B. Yeats: "A figure in a dark cape. I said, 'Are you the poet, Mr. Yeats?' He stopped, raised his hand high and said, 'I yām.'"

But these matters were of the past and I had said a temporary good-bye to Revisson Doe on signature of the contract. *Warrender Chase* was to be published some time in May or early June, and I only had to wait for the proofs. At the end of January when I went back to my work at Sir Quentin's I had almost obliterated the book from my thoughts.

The proofs came at the end of March, and when I came face to face with my *Warrender Chase* again I was so far estranged from it that I couldn't bring myself to look through the proofs for typographical errors. Instead I went with Solly one afternoon to St. John's Wood to see our friends Theo and Audrey, a married couple who had both published their first novels and who consequently enjoyed a little more respect, in that very hierarchical literary world, than did my unpublished friends whom I used to meet at poetry readings at the Ethical Church Hall. Theo and Audrey had agreed to read my proofs for me. I exhorted them to make no changes but only to look for spelling errors.

I handed over my proofs.

These were kind people. "You look haunted," said Theo. "What's the matter with you?"

"She is haunted," said Solly.

"I am haunted," I said, but I wouldn't explain any further. Solly said, "Her job's getting her down," and left it at that.

Audrey made me up a package of buns and sandwiches left over from tea, to take home.

Since the end of January and for the past two months I had come to feel that the members of Sir Quentin's group resembled more and more the bombed-out buildings that still messed up the London street-scene. These ruins were getting worse, month by month, and so were the Auto-biographical people.

Dottie couldn't see it.

Sir Eric Findlay said to me, "Do you *really* think Mrs. Wilks is in her right mind?"

I thought it safest to say, "What is a right mind?" He looked frightened. We were alone having coffee after lunch in the ladies' sitting-room of the Bath Club which, because of a fire in its original premises, was housed within another club, I think the Conservative.

"What is a right mind? Well, you have a right mind, Fleur, and everyone knows it. The point is that the Hallam Street set are saying . . . Don't you think it's time we all had it out with each other? One big row would be better than the way we're going on."

I said that I didn't care for the idea of one big row.

Sir Eric waved his hand in mild greeting to a

middle-aged couple who had just come in and who sat down on a sofa at the other end of the room. Other people presently joined them. Sir Eric waved and nodded across the room in his timid way as if making a side-gesture to some sweet discourse with me about the London Philharmonic, the Cheltenham Gold Cup or even my own charms, instead of this depressing conversation about what was wrong with the Autobiographical Association. I longed for the power of the Evil Eye so that I could cast it on Eric Findlay in revenge for his taking me out to lunch and then assaulting me with his kinky complaints.

"One big row," he said, his timid little eyes glinting. "Mrs. Wilks is not in her right mind but you, Fleur, are in your right mind," he said, as if there was some question that I wasn't.

I felt some panic which however I knew I could control. I felt I should sit on quietly as one would in the sudden presence of a dangerous beast. The atmosphere of my *Warrender Chase* came back to me, but grotesquely, without its even-tempered tone. When I first started writing people used to say my novels were exaggerated. They never were exaggerated, merely aspects of realism. Sir Eric Findlay was real, sitting there on the sofa by my side complaining how Mrs. Wilks had failed to appreciate the latest part of his autobiography, his war record, and thus was out of her mind. All Mrs. Wilks could think of, he said, was the foolish incident in his schooldays with another boy while thinking of an actress. "Mrs. Wilks harps on it," said Eric.

"You shouldn't have revealed it. Those autobiographies are dangerous," I said.

"Well, a lot of them were your doing, Fleur," he said.

"Not the dangerous passages. Only the funny parts."

"Sir Quentin insists," he said, "on complete frankness. Are you leaving that sugar?" He pointed to a tiny lump of sugar on the saucer of my coffee-cup. I said I didn't want it. He put it in his pocket in a small envelope he kept for the purpose. "They say it will be off the ration in three months," he said in an excited whisper.

Dottie said to me that evening, "I quite see Eric's point of view. Mrs. Wilks has an obsession about sex. I don't believe she was raped by a Russian soldier before she escaped. It's wishful thinking."

"It makes no difference to me what any of you did," I said. "I just can't stand all the gossip, the canvassing, the lobbying, among the awful members."

"Sir Quentin insists on complete frankness and I think we should all be frank with each other," Dottie said.

I looked at her, I know, as if she were a complete stranger.

Maisie Young had found out where I lived. She

had come to my room, one Saturday afternoon, only some days before I met Sir Eric Findlay at his club for lunch. She had come complaining too, as it turned out, although she at first protested she didn't want to come in, she only wanted to leave me a book and she had kept the taxi waiting. We sent the taxi away.

"Oh," said Maisie, "what a delightful little wee room, so compact." She herself came out of the best half of a house in Portman Square and enjoyed the rent of the other half. I think Maisie was rather stunned at the spacelessness of this room where I lived all of my present life, she was amazed that anyone could have space for intelligent ideas when they lived with a gas ring for cooking, a bed for sitting and sleeping on, an orange box for food stores and plates, a table for eating and writing on, a wash-basin for washing at, two chairs for sitting on or (as on the present occasion), hanging washing on, a corner cupboard for clothes, walls to hold shelves of books and a floor on which one stepped over more books, set in piles. All this Maisie, clutching her bag like a horse's rein, took in with a dazed look-round as if she had been thrown from her horse yet again. I believe it was out of sheer kindness that she kept on saying, "Compact, compact, it's really . . . it's really . . . I didn't know they had this sort of thing."

I bundled the washing off one of the chairs and settled Maisie into it with two volumes of the *Encyclopaedia Britannica* and the complete Chaucer piled up for a footstool whereon to rest her poor caged leg, as I always did for Edwina and for Solly Mendelsohn when they came to see me. She took this very kindly. I sat on the bed and smiled.

"I mean, I didn't know they had this sort of thing in Kensington," said Maisie. "I mean in Kensington nowadays. Is this where you bring Lady Edwina?"

I said yes, sometimes. I set about making tea, so much to the renewed astonishment of Maisie in Wonderland that I felt bound to assure her that I often had quite a lot of visitors, five, six, even more, at a time.

"How do you keep so clean, yourself?" said Maisie, looking at me with new eyes.

"There's a bathroom on every landing. A bath is fourpence a time."

"Is that all?"

"It's too much," I said, and explained how the proprietors made a fortune out of the penny gas meters in the bathrooms and the shilling meters in the rooms, since they got a refund when the meter-man came to collect, which refunded loot was not shared among the clients.

"I suppose," said Maisie, "they have to make some sort of a profit." I could see whose side she was on and although she then looked round the room enquiringly I didn't enlighten her as to the rent, lest she should exclaim over its dirt-cheapness.

"What a lot of books—have you read them all?" she said.

Still, I liked her very much. She was merely

91

ignorant about penniless realities, as indeed she was about most realities, but she wasn't pretentious. Maisie settled down with her tea and biscuit and started saying what she had come to say.

"Father Egbert Delaney," said this handsome girl, "believes that Satan is a woman. He told me as much and I think he ought to be made to resign. It's an insult to women."

"It does seem so," I said. "Why don't you tell him?"

"I think you, as secretary, Fleur, should take it up with him and report the matter to Sir Quentin."

"But if I tell him Satan is a man he'll think it an insult to men."

She said, "Personally, I don't believe in Satan."

"Well that's all right then," I said.

"What's all right then?"

"If Satan doesn't exist, why bother if it's man or woman we're talking about?"

"It's Father Delaney we're talking about. Do you know what I think?"

I said, what did she think?

"Father Delaney is Satan. Satan himself. You should report the whole thing to Sir Quentin. Sir Quentin insists on complete frankness. It's time we had a show-down."

I still liked Maisie Young, she had an air of freedom that she wasn't herself aware of, and she reminded me as she sat there in my room of my character Marjorie in *Warrender Chase*. But I didn't dwell on this at the time; I was thinking of her phrase "Sir Quentin insists on complete frankness." It stuck in my mind so that, a few days later when I sat with Eric Findlay in his club and he twice spoke that very phrase, I was convinced that Sir Quentin Oliver had started orchestrating his band of fools. At the moment, sitting with Maisie in my room I was simply irritated by her "Sir Quentin insists." I said, "Complete frankness is always a mistake among friends."

"I know what you mean," said Maisie. "You make out you're happy to see me but really you don't like me coming here. I'm only a cripple and a bore to you."

I was appalled, for the moment that she had turned my generality on to herself, she indeed became a very great bore, not merely for the present hour, but stretching into the future; this apprehension of Maisie in the future affected me with a clutching void in my stomach. All in a moment she had seemed to lose that air of a freedom that she would probably never be aware existed.

I said, "Oh, Maisie, I had no such thing in mind. I spoke generally. Frankness is usually a euphemism for rudeness."

"People should be frank," said the wretched girl. "I know I'm a cripple and a bore."

I longed for the telephone to ring but it didn't, or someone else to come in, but just at that moment nobody did. I murmured something to the effect that a physical disability often proved to be an attraction. She replied sharply that she'd rather not discuss her sex-life. So much for my frankness.

Now Maisie lifted up the book she had brought me. It was the copy of John Henry Newman's *Apologia pro Vita Sua* that I had borrowed from the public library for her. "Sir Quentin has lent me a copy of his own," said Maisie. She was looking at me without really noticing my presence. For a moment I felt like a grey figment, the "I" of a novel whose physical description the author had decided not to set forth. I was still, of course, weak from my 'flu. She flicked through the pages of the *Apologia* and found a bit she wanted to read aloud to me. It was the passage, early in the book, where Newman describes his religious feelings as a boy. He felt he was elected to eternal glory. He said the actual belief gradually faded away but that it had an influence on the opinions of his early youth:

> . . . viz. in isolating me from the objects which surrounded me, in confirming me in my mistrust of the reality of material phenomena, and making me rest in the thought of two and two only supreme and luminously self-evident beings, myself and my Creator. . . .

Maisie finished reading. She said, "I think that is very, very beautiful and so true."

Now I got angry. I was impatient with the force of having spent the past three and a half years studying Newman, his sermons, his essays, his life, his theology, and I had done it for no reward, and at the sacrifice of pleasures and happiness which would never come my way again, while Maisie up to the time of her accident had been spending her time at deb dances, riding in the parks of such country-houses as had been restored by the government to their owners after the war, and, since her accident, plotting out with her friends her totally undisciplined theories of the Cosmos. The sacrifice of pleasures is of course itself a pleasure, but I didn't feel up to such pure reasoning at the time; Maisie's reading me this well-known passage of Newman and telling me it was beautiful and true irritated me greatly. I said, "Newman is describing a passing phase."

"Oh, no," said Maisie, "it goes through and through his book. Two and two only supreme and luminously self-evident beings, my Creator and myself."

Suddenly I knew there was a sense in which she was right and the whole Newman idea which up to now I had thought enchanting took on a different aspect. I had always up to now had a particular liking for this passage, feeling a fierce conviction of its power and general application as a human ideal. But as Maisie uttered the words I felt a revulsion against an awful madness I then discerned in it. ". . . My mistrust of material phenomena . . . two and two only supreme and luminously self-evident beings, my Creator and myself." I was glad of my strong hips and sound cage of ribs to save me from flying apart, so explosive were my thoughts. But I heard myself saying, coldly, "It's quite a neurotic view of life. It's a poetic vision only. Newman was a nineteenth-century romantic."

"Do you know," she said, "there are still people alive who remember Cardinal Newman. He was considered to be an angel."

"I think it awful," I said, "to contemplate a world in which there are only two luminous and self-evident beings, your creator and yourself. You shouldn't read Newman in that way."

"It's a beautiful thought, a very beautiful—"

"I'm sorry I ever told you to read the *Apologia*. It's a beautiful piece of poetic paranoia." This was over-simple, a distortion; but I needed the rhetoric to combat the girl's ideas.

"Father Egbert Delaney mentioned it to me first," she said. "I don't know how that evil fellow can possibly appreciate the book. But it's true you also pressed us all to read it as an example of an autobiography."

"For my part Father Egbert Delaney is a self-evident and luminous being," I said. "So are you, so is my lousy landlord and the same goes for everyone I know. You can't live with an I-and-thou relationship to God and doubt the reality of the rest of life."

"Have you told Sir Quentin about your views?" Maisie said. "Because," she said, "Sir Quentin insists on complete frankness. He has told us we are all to study the *Apologia* as an example of autobiographical writing."

By this time I had calmed down and I was

thinking how much unpaid overtime I had saved myself by failing to remind them of Proust and his fictional autobiography. I wanted to get rid of Maisie and forget the Autobiographical Association for the week-end at least. Those people and their Sir Quentin were sheets of paper on which I could write short stories, poems, anything I cared. Orgulous and impatient I told Maisie while looking at my watch that I had to make a phone call—"Goodness, the time!"—I moved with these words to the telephone and put through a call to Dottie's number. She wasn't in. I put down the receiver and said to Maisie, who surprisingly had given no indication of leaving, "I'm afraid I've missed my friend."

She was looking straight ahead as if struck by catalepsy, and oblivious of my phoning and fussing. I thought she had been taken badly, but then she spoke in a trance-like way that made me suspect that it was all put on. "Father Egbert Delaney is Satan personified. You'll believe me when I tell you what he said about you, Fleur."

I was instantly agog. "What—did—he—say—about—me?"

She went into another dream-like state. I knew I was being foolish to press her for more, but I was dying to know.

At last she spoke: "Your Father Egbert Delaney whom you're so anxious to protect says that you are trying to persuade Lady Edwina to change her will in your favour. He says Beryl Tims is convinced of it. In fact, many of the others are convinced of it."

I laughed, but the laughter was artificial, which I hoped didn't show.

"Father Egbert Delaney," she said, "says, why else should you bother to take the awful old crone out for walks and spend so much time with her?"

I prayed for someone to phone me or look in to see me. That my prayer appeared to be answered within a very short time is no proof of its efficacy; it was six o'clock, a time when any of my friends might ring me up or stop to see me on their way somewhere. Maisie was saying, "It's a question that's bound to arise, isn't it? Of course I think Egbert Delaney is thoroughly evil. I'm on your side in this, Fleur, and I don't think you need, really, explain why you give so much attention to that disgusting woman."

"I need not even explain why I give so much attention to you," I said. "I daresay you'll die before me but I don't expect you to leave me anything in your will."

"Oh, Fleur, that's harsh, that's brutal of you. How can you speak like that? How can you think of me dying? And I'm on your side, on your side, and I only told you for your own—"

A knock at the door. It opened, and to my surprise Leslie's poet, who was so literally called Gray Mauser that he wrote under the pseudonym of Leander put his timid head round the door. Gray had only been to see me once before. I said, "Oh, Gray, I'm so glad to see you. Come in!"

He looked very much encouraged by my welcome. In came the self-evident and luminous little mess. He was small, slight and wispy, about twenty, with arms and legs not quite uncoordinated enough to qualify him for any sort of medical treatment, and yet definitely he was not put together right. I couldn't have been happier to see him.

"I only just wondered if perhaps by chance Leslie was here," said Gray.

"Oh, I daresay he'll be along in a moment," I said. I introduced him to Maisie and quickly said she would no doubt be grateful if Gray nipped out to get her a taxi.

He lolloped off to do so immediately, glad to be of help. I followed with Maisie, helping her with her stick and the straps of her handbag twined round her fingers. She was probably upset but I didn't care to verify it one way or another. I got her into the taxi at the door and went back in, shivering with the cold, followed by Leslie's poet.

That evening we went off to a pub known for its literary clients where we drank light ale and ate Cornish pasties; in mine, I counted two small diced cubes of steak, Gray found but one among the small bits of potato nestling inside the tough envelope of pastry. And this I find most curious: looking back on it the idea of that Cornish pasty, day-old as it was, is to me revolting but at the time it was delicious; and so I ask, what did I see in that lard-laden Cornish pasty?—in much the same way as I might wonder, now, whatever was the attraction of a man like Leslie?

I sat with Gray at a lone table of the pub. There

99

were one or two well-known poets at the bar at whom we glanced from our respectful distance, for they were far beyond our sphere. I think the poets at the bar on that occasion were Dylan Thomas and Roy Campbell, or it could have been Louis Mac-Neice and someone else; it made no difference for the point was we felt that the atmosphere was as good as the Cornish pasties and beer, and we could talk. Gray told me about his many troubles. Leslie had gone to Ireland with Dottie three days ago, had promised to be back last night but hadn't turned up. He had left Gray a consolation present of a grey silk tie with blue spots which Gray was wearing and which he seemed both proud of and saddened by. I had very little to say to Gray Mauser but I remember that sitting with him in the pub that night took the edge off my rage against Maisie Young. I cheered him up by saying that I didn't really think Leslie was a lady's man. We decided that men were generally more sentimental than women, but women generally more dependable. Then he took some sheets of crumpled paper out of his pocket and read me a poem about the sickle moon which he explained was a sexual symbol.

I had never thought highly of Gray, there was so little to think anything of. But just that evening, after we parted and I was on my way home in the Tube, I thought how sane he was compared with Maisie and the Autobiographical Association in general. When I got out at High Street Kensington

it was raining and cold, and I went on my way
rejoicing.

So that, a few days later when I had to sit in his
club listening to Sir Eric Findlay's complaints, I was
somewhat prepared; I was able to control my
panic.

Chapter Six

When Dottie came back from Ireland the following week-end, a week later than expected, Leslie
again deserted her for Gray. "I wouldn't mind so
much," Dottie said when she came to see me, "but
to be abandoned in favour of that little rat is more
than I can stand. If he was at least an attractive boy,
or bright, intelligent . . . But he's so pathetic, that
Gray Mauser!"

I pointed out to Dottie that Leslie had by no
means moved from herself to Gray. "It was I whom
he left," I said.

"I didn't mind sharing with you," Dottie said. I
laughed. Dottie, in turn, thought it odd that I
should find the situation amusing.

"Of course," said the English Rose, "you're hard
and I'm soft. Leslie brings me his work to type, and
like a fool I do it. He's writing a novel." She had
taken out her knitting.

I enquired eagerly about the novel. She said she
couldn't tell me anything except the title *Two Ways*.
I speculated to myself merrily about the variety of
themes the title might fit. "Leslie will no doubt let
you see it, himself, when it's finished," Dottie said.
"It's very good, very deep."

"Is it autobiographical?" I enquired.

"Oh, yes, basically," Dottie said with some pride, as if this was a prime requisite of a good, deep novel. "Of course he's changed the names. But it's a very frank novel, which is all that matters in the world of to-day. Sir Quentin, for instance, always insists on complete frankness."

I didn't want to upset Dottie or I would have laid down my conviction that complete frankness is not a quality that favours art. Then she said, sadly, that no one was ever completely frank, it was an illusion. I said I agreed, and this made her uneasy.

But in any case I was weary of the sound of Sir Quentin's name and all the twanging of harps round his throne.

I told her about my visit from Maisie. I told her about my lunch with Eric Findlay. I realized after a while that Dottie was unusually silent. None the less I went on. I added the detail (which was true) that, while sitting on the low sofa at Eric Findlay's club, side by side with him, he had crossed his legs in such a way that the sole of his shoe was almost in my face; I said that it was unconsciously at least a desire to insult. I told Dottie that I thought Newman's *Apologia* was the wrong book to have introduced into the group, treating as it did of a special case, Newman's self-defence against Charles Kingsley's accusations of insincerity; I said the autobiographies were taking on a paranoiac turn as a consequence of following the *Apologia*. I said a far better model would be the *Life* of Cellini, robust and full-blooded as it was. A touch of normality, I said. Dottie knitted on.

She knitted on. It was a red wool scarf; she frequently came to the end of the row, turning her knitting again and again. I told her that Sir Quentin was conforming more and more to the character of my Warrender Chase; it was amazing, I could have invented him, I could have invented all of them—the lot. I said Edwina was the only real person out of the whole collection. Dottie stopped her knitting for a moment at this and looked at me. She said nothing, then she went on knitting.

And I went on talking without once inviting a response. Her silence didn't seem immediately remarkable to me; indeed I felt that I was making a strong impression. I told her that the whole Auto-biographical set were in my opinion becoming unhinged to the satisfaction of Sir Quentin, and I concluded by recounting something that Father Egbert Delaney had muttered to me at a meeting, it was a deprecatory phrase about "Mrs. Wilks's tits"; this, I informed Dottie, was an offence to me, even more than to Mrs. Wilks. Vulgarity, I explained, I could take from Solly Mendelsohn or, if he had been alive to-day, the sixteenth-century Benvenuto Cellini, because these were big sane men, but I wasn't going to let that Creeping Jesus of a *défroqué* get thrills out of insulting my ear.

"It's getting late," Dottie said. She put away her knitting in her awful black bag, said good-night and left.

105

When she was gone, struck by her silence, I gave it a new interpretation. I gave her time to get home and phoned her.

"Was there anything the matter, Dottie?"

"Look," she said, "I think you're unhinged. You're suffering from delusions. There's nothing the matter with us. We're a perfectly normal group. I think there's something the matter with you. Beryl Tims—well, I'll let her speak for herself. Your *Warrender Chase* is a thoroughly sick novel. Theo and Audrey Clairmont think it's sick, it worried them terribly, correcting the proofs. Leslie says it's mad."

I pulled myself together sufficiently to think of a retort suitable to the occasion, since it was the attack on my *Warrender Chase* that really annoyed me; I didn't care about the rest.

"If you have any influence with Leslie in the matter of his novel," I drawled in the calmness of my suppressed hysteria, "you might get him to eliminate that dreadful recurrent phrase of his, 'With regard to. . . .' He uses it all the time in his reviews."

I could hear Dottie crying. I meant to tell her more about Leslie's prose, its frightful tautology. He never reached the point until it was undetectably lost in a web of multisyllabic words and images trowelled on like cement.

She said, "You didn't say this when you were sleeping with him."

"I didn't sleep with him for his prose style."

106

"I think," said Dottie, "you're out of your element in our world."

So ended one of my million, as it seemed, rows with Dottie.

"Oh, Fleur!" said Lady Bernice "Bucks" Gilbert in her hoarse drawl, "would you mind handing round the sandwiches? You could also help with the coats; my little maid has only one pair of hands. See if anyone needs a drink . . ." She had pressed me to come to her cocktail party, and here I was in her flat in Curzon Street in my blue velvet dress among a crowd of chatterers. I now saw why she had pressed the invitation so hard. Half-heartedly I lifted a plate of cheese biscuits and put it under the nose of a solid-looking young man standing by me.

He took a biscuit and said, "Fleur, it's you."

It was Wally McConnachie, an old friend of mine from war-time who worked in the Foreign Office. Wally had been in Canada. We lolled against the wallpaper and talked while Bucks glared at me in a somewhat ugly way. When she had glared enough and I had got back my smile with Wally's talk and a drink, I roped in Wally to take people's coats at the door and to help me in pushing the sandwiches, which were filled with black-market delicacies and of which Wally and I ate our share. This infuriated Bucks the more.

"I'm sure," she said, as she passed me by, "that

Sir Quentin would want you to help. He hasn't arrived yet."

I said that Sir Quentin insisted on perfect frankness and to be quite frank I was helping, and the sandwiches were a great success.

Presently Sir Quentin arrived and one by one the members of the Autobiographical Association filtered in among the other guests. The room was packed. I saw Dottie talking earnestly to Maisie while looking over at me. Empty glasses stood all over the grand piano on which was a large photograph of Bucks's late and hyper-bemedalled husband. My hostess caught my arm and silently pointed to the glasses.

Wally and I collected them, dumped them in the kitchen and made our get-away. We dined at Prunier's with its tranquillizing aquarium-decor, while we described the lives we had been leading since last we had met. The fish swam and darted in their element, while we talked and looked into each other's eyes a lot over our wine. We went on to Quaglino's, whose decor then was picture frames without any pictures on the dark walls, and we danced till four in the morning.

Wally told me numerous amusing stories in the course of the evening. They were very weightless stories but for that very reason I felt restored. For instance he told me about a girl he had met who had an uncanny habit of sneezing if she drank inferior wine, and as a consequence of this talent got a job with a wine-merchandising firm as a taster. He told me about another girl whose mother, to overcome her daughter's strong objections to marrying some man on the grounds that he had chronic bad breath, said, "Well you can't have *everything.*" Such blithe anecdotes put me in a frame of mind to see myself once more in a carefree light. I told a number of funny stories to Wally about Sir Quentin's set at Hallam Street, and I gave him an outline of what my life was like on the grubby edge of the literary world. Wally, who was racking his brains as to where he had heard of old Quentin Oliver "somewhere or other," and was extremely entertained by my stories, at the same time advised me strongly to get another job. "I should get out of all that if I were you, Fleur. You'd be happier."

I said yes, possibly. In fact, it came to me during that evening of high spirits that I preferred to stay in the job; I preferred to be interested as I was than happy as I might be. I wasn't sure that I so much wanted to be happy, but I knew I had to follow my nature. However, I didn't say this to Wally. It wouldn't have done.

I promised Wally that he should meet the fabulous Edwina.

I stayed in bed next morning; about eleven o'clock, when I woke, I telephoned to Hallam Street to say I wasn't coming in.

Beryl Tims answered the phone.

"Have you got a medical certificate?" she said.

"Go to hell."

"Pardon?"

109

"I'm not ill," I said. "I was out dancing all night, that's all."

"Hold on while I get Sir Quentin."

"I can't," I said. "There's somebody at my door."

This was true; I hung up and went to find at the door the red-faced house-boy with a bunch of amber-coloured roses and behind him the daily cleaner, whose unwanted services were thrown in with the rent, in her pink dress and white apron. It was a colourful ensemble. I stared at them for a moment, then I sent the maid away while the house-boy told me that I'd had a visitor the night before— "That awful nice lady that's married to your gentleman friend. I let her in here to wait, and she waited the best part of an hour. 'Twas after ten she left." I gathered this was Dottie.

I got rid of the boy and counted the roses, which were from Wally. Fourteen. This pleased me. I always liked getting roses, but the usual dozen seemed always so shop-ordered. Fourteen had been really thought of.

In the late afternoon, at about six, when I was thinking of getting up and doing a bit of my new novel, the Baronne Clotilde du Loiret rang me up. "Sir Quentin," she said, "is worried about you, Fleur. Are you indisposed? Sir Quentin thought there might be something I could do. If you have any problem, you know, Sir Quentin insists on complete frankness."

"I'm taking a day off. How good of Sir Quentin to be so concerned."

"But just at this moment, Fleur, as I say, the

affairs of the Association are falling to bits, aren't they? I mean, Bucks Gilbert is a bit much, isn't she? Of course, she hasn't a penny. I mean, we all had a very frank discussion this afternoon. I've just left them. Then Quentin introduced a sort of prayer-meeting, my dear, it was most embarrassing. What could one do? I quite see that I for one have a private life and when I say private life, I'm sure you know what I mean. But I do object to being prayed over. Do you know, I'm terrified of Quentin. He knows too much. And Maisie Young—"

"Why don't you give it up?" I said.

"What? Our Autobiographical Association? Well, I can't explain, but I do believe in Quentin. I'm sure you do too, Fleur."

"Oh, yes. I almost feel I invented him."

"Fleur, do you think there's something, I mean something special, between him and Beryl Tims? I mean, they're very thick with each other. And you know, this afternoon at the prayer part, that awful Mummy of Quentin's came in and started making that sort of insinuation. Of course she's ga-ga, but one wonders. She says she's fond of you, Fleur, and I think Quentin is rather worried about that too. And I mean, is it true you've written a novel about us, Fleur?"

Chapter Seven

I have the impression that I was tuning into voices without really hearing them as one does when moving from programme to programme on a wireless set. I know there was a lot of activity at Hallam Street. Eric Findlay and Dottie ganged up against Mrs. Wilks, arriving at Hallam Street together one morning when Sir Quentin was out at the local Food office trying vainly to get extra tea and sugar rations on behalf of the Association. I remember plainly on that occasion Dottie asking me irrelevantly if I had heard from my publishers. I said I had received a printed acknowledgement of the proofs and now I was waiting for publication. Dottie said, "Oh!"

Another day came Mrs. Wilks in her pastel hues, and her veils, and a wet purple umbrella which she refused to give up to Beryl Tims. She had lost her fat, merry look. I had noticed the last time I saw her that she was losing weight, but now it was quite obvious she had either been very ill or was on a diet. Her painted-up face was shrivelled, making her nose too long; her eyes were big and inexactly focused. She demanded that I change her name in the records from Mrs. Wilks to Miss Davids, explaining that she had to be *incognito* from now on since the Trotskyites were posting agents all over the world to find and assassinate her. I remember that Sir Quentin came in while she was raving thus, and sent me out on an errand. When I came back Mrs. Wilks was gone and Sir Quentin was leaning back in his chair, eyes half-closed, with that one shoulder of his slightly in advance of the other and his hands clasped before him as if in prayer. I was about to ask what had been the matter with Mrs. Wilks when he said, "Mrs. Wilks has been fasting too strictly." Whereupon he turned to something else. He was very much on the defensive about his little flock. One day, about this time, I made some scornful remark to Sir Quentin about Father Egbert Delaney who had been remonstrating with me on the telephone about Edwina's presence at the meetings. Sir Quentin replied loftily, "One of his ancestors fought in the Battle of Bosworth Field."

My job at Sir Quentin's, now that he had taken the actual autobiographies out of my hands, was taken up largely with Sir Quentin's other, quite normal, private and business affairs. He seemed to dictate unnecessary letters to old friends, some of which I suspect he never sent, since he would often put them aside to sign and post himself. I felt sure he now wanted to establish the idea of his normality in my mind. He apparently had business interests in South Africa, for he wrote about them. His villa at Grasse was greatly on his mind, it having been occupied by the Germans during the war; he was anxious only to find out by which

Germans. "Members of the High Command and the Old Guard I have no doubt." He had an interest in a paint manufacturers who were compiling a history of the firm, *One Hundred Prosperous Years;* I helped with the dreary proofs. I doubted if he needed me at all, except that I was useful in coping with the members when they took to dropping in or telephoning as they now did more and more phrenetically.

It was about this time that he said to me, "What have you got against the *Apologia?*"

I forget how I answered him precisely. It was something indirect and casual. I wasn't at any event about to be drawn into a discussion of that exquisite work or any other with Sir Quentin. All I wanted to know was what he was up to. And besides, I had been thinking about autobiographies in general. From the personal reminiscences of the members I had perceived that anecdotes and memoirs are only valuable if they are extremely unusual in themselves, or if they attach to an interesting end-product. The boyhood experiences of Newman or of Michelangelo would be interesting, however trivial, but who cared—who should care—about Eric Findlay's memories of his butler and nanny, he being what Sir Eric Findlay was? It was precisely because I'd found all their biographies so very dull to start with that I'd given them so light-hearted a turn, almost as if the events they described had happened to me, not to them. At least I did them the honour of treating their output as life-stories not as case-histories for psycho-

115

analysis, as they more or less were; I had set them on to writing fictions about themselves.

Now these autobiographies were out of my hands; but I didn't care; they were dreary, one and all.

I was sure that nothing had happened in their lives and equally sure that Sir Quentin was pumping something artificial into their real lives instead of on paper. Presented fictionally, one could have done something authentic with that poor material. But the inducing them to express themselves in life resulted in falsity.

What is truth? I could have realized these people with my fun and games with their life-stories, while Sir Quentin was destroying them with his needling after frankness. When people say that nothing happens in their lives I believe them. But you must understand that everything happens to an artist; time is always redeemed, nothing is lost and wonders never cease.

It wasn't till much later that I found he was handing out to all of them, including Dottie, small yellow pills called Dexedrine which he told them would enable them to endure the purifying fasts he inflicted. The pills were no part of my *Warrender Chase;* Sir Quentin thought of them himself, doubting his power to enthrall unaided.

Now, on that same day as he asked me this question about the *Apologia* Sir Quentin switched over to the problem of his mother. "Mummy," he said, "is a problem."

116

I busied myself placing a sheet of carbon paper between a sheet of writing paper and one of copy paper.

"Mummy," he said, "has always been a problem. And I want to tell you, Miss Talbot, that you would do well to ignore any promises Mummy might have effected in your regard as to an eventual legacy. She is probably senile. Mrs. Tims and I—"

"The noun 'promise' is not generally followed by the verb 'effected,'" I put in wildly, trying to keep calm. I had seen while he was speaking that he pressed the bell for Mrs. Tims. As the door-bell rang at that moment she didn't immediately appear, but Sir Quentin smiled at my little divergence and went on, "I know you have been very good to Mummy, taking her out on Sundays, and I'm sure that if you have been out of pocket we can find ways and means of reimbursement. There is no question but that if you care to continue some little arrangement can be made. It is only that, for the future—"

"For the future I'm well provided for, thank you," I slammed in. "And for the past, present and future I don't take payment for friendship."

"You have matrimonial prospects?" he said.

I went berserk. I said, "I have written a novel that's going to be a success. It's to be published in May." I don't know why I said this, except that I was beside myself with rage. In reality I had no hopes of success of any kind for my *Warrender Chase*. The new novel I was working on—my

117

second, my *All Souls' Day*— occupied my best brains now, my sweetest hopes. I thought that *Warrender Chase* might do respectably well as an introduction to my second book. I didn't know then, as I know now, that it's always the book I am working on that takes precedence in my esteem.

However, I was in no mood for the delicacies of my own opinions at that moment when out I spat the words, "I have written a novel . . ."

"Now my dear Miss Talbot, let us be perfectly frank. Don't you think you've had delusions of grandeur?"

I perceived four things simultaneously: Beryl Tims came hammering with her heels, and opening the door, simpered that Lady Bernice was waiting; Sir Quentin opened the deep right-hand drawer of his desk with a smile; and, still at the same time, I was rehearing his words, "Don't you think you've had delusions of grandeur?" which all in a mental moment I noticed was a use of the past tense—why didn't he say, ". . . you're having delusions . . ."?—and finally as the fourth element in this total set of impressions I recognized that his words "Don't you think you've had delusions of grandeur?" were the very words of my Warrender Chase; in his letter to my fictional English Rose, Charlotte, when he advises her how to question Marjorie, he actually writes, "Put it to her like this: 'Don't you think you've had delusions of grandeur?' And then when my ancient Prudence is trying to recall to my scholar Proudie what happened about the Greek girl at the prayer-meeting who later committed suicide, I make my Prudence say, "Oh, Warrender was aware she was in a very bad way. Only a few days before he had said to her, 'Don't you think you've had delusions of grandeur?'"

I noticed these four things together, still fuming as I was. I think my fury had put me in a state of heightened perception, for standing up to go I caught a glimpse into the drawer Sir Quentin had opened. In a flash he had shut it again. Now, in the drawer I had seen a bundle of galley proofs, and by the light of reason I should have assumed they were those from the Settlebury Paint Company, founded 1850, their centenary book. I only had a distant and quick glimpse of the folded proofs in the drawer. I wasn't near enough to identify the type-face or the spacing or any of the words. Why then did it go through me that those were the proofs of my *Warrender Chase?* The thought went through me but I let it go, remembering about the paint people. Sir Quentin's two sets of proofs were about equal to one set of my novel.

It all happened very quickly. I stood, furious with Sir Quentin, ready to walk out. Beryl Tims hovered for instructions and Sir Quentin, when he had shut the drawer, said, "Sit down, Mrs. Tims. Miss Talbot, be seated a moment." I refused to be seated. I said, "I'm leaving." I noticed that Beryl Tims was wearing the brooch I had given her; she fingered it and said, "Shall I tell Lady Bernice—"

119

"Mrs. Tims," said Sir Quentin, "let me inform you that you are in the presence of an authoress."

"Pardon?"

"An authoress of a best-selling novel."

"Lady Bernice seems to be very upset. She must see you, Sir Quentin. I said—"

By this time I had gathered my things and had left the room. Out bounded Sir Quentin after me. "My dear Miss Talbot you mustn't, you simply mustn't leave. I spoke for the best. Mummy would be devastated. Mrs. Tims—I ask you—Miss Talbot has taken offence."

I said good-night and went off, too enraged to speak. But as I left I saw Lady Bernice standing in the doorway of the drawing room with a really distraught look on her face, not at all her dominant self; she was dressed-up as usual but the glimpse I got as I passed her by impressed on me the picture of fashionable clothes all awry and make-up daubed and smeared about her eyes. It was the last time I ever saw her. I heard Sir Quentin say, "Why, Bucks, whatever . . ." just as I left, and I was far too wrapped up in my own grievances to dwell on that last look which imprinted itself on my mind so that I can see it now.

I was anxious to get home and was still amazed at my stupidity in making that large prophecy for my *Warrender Chase,* and I wondered where the words had come from, ". . . a novel that's going to be a success." I had placed myself at the man's mercy by saying this; not that I regarded success as a disgrace, but that I wasn't thinking of *Warrender*

Chase in that light just then, and also, I had known for a long time that success could not be my profession in life, nor failure a calling for that matter. These were by-products. Why, then, I was asking myself all the way home, had I fallen into Sir Quentin's trap? For that was how I saw it. He had been able, then, to bring out those very words of Warrender Chase, "Don't you think you've had delusions of grandeur?"

I had put away my copy of *Warrender Chase*. It was my manuscript copy, written on foolscap pages, from which I had typed the copy that went to the publishers. I hadn't taken a carbon copy of the typescript, not seeing any point in wasting paper. But I had made a parcel of my manuscript, marked it on the outside, "Warrender Chase by Fleur Talbot" and put it on the floor of my clothes cupboard.

When I got home, to make sure I wasn't mistaken about Sir Quentin's use of Warrender's actual words, I decided to get the book out and look up the two passages. I was in a flutter, feeling partly that I had in fact some delusions of grandeur or of persecution or some other symptom of paranoia. I couldn't have felt more paranoiac when I discovered that my copy of *Warrender Chase* was not in the cupboard where it should have been. The package, about the dimensions of a London telephone directory, was not there.

I started to search my room. I began by absurdly turning things over, the new pages of my current work, *All Soul's Day*, included. No sign of *Warrender*

Chase. I sat down and thought. Nothing came of my frantic thinking. I got up and started to tidy the room very carefully, very meticulously, shifting every piece of furniture, every book. I did it all rather slowly, moving everything first into the middle of the room, then moving everything back, piece by piece, book by book; pencils, typewriter, food-stores, everything. This activity was pure superstition, for it was obvious at a few glances that the package was not in the room, but so minute was my search I might have been looking for a lost diamond. I found many lost things, old letters, half-a-crown, old poems and stories but no *Warrender Chase*. I opened every other package that I had pushed into an old suitcase: nothing.

I poured some whisky into a tumbler, in a very careful and stunned manner, added some water from the tap, and sat sipping it. The cleaning woman must have thrown it out. But how? It had been left in the cupboard. She had worked in the place for years, she never opened people's cupboards or drawers, never took anything. Besides, I had always asked her to be careful about my papers and packages and she always had been careful, not even dusting the table my work was lying on lest she should disarrange it. She grumbled so much about the mess in my room she hardly flicked a duster anywhere. I started going over in my mind who had been in my room since last I had seen *Warrender Chase* in the cupboard. Wally had been briefly but only to pick me up to go out somewhere one evening. I thought, could the Alexanders have come rummaging? That was absurd. Leslie? Dottie? I passed them all over, forgetting completely for the moment that Dottie had in fact been in my room during my absence that first evening I went dancing at Quaglino's with Wally. But I didn't think of this till later. At the time I sat and wondered if I were going mad, if *Warrender Chase* existed or had I imagined the book.

I took up the phone to ring Wally. The switchboard was off; I saw it was already nearly midnight.

But the very act of thinking about Wally put me to rights; it didn't matter so very much after all what had happened to my manuscript. The typescript and the proofs were safely with the publishers. I could get back my typescript from Revisson Doe.

I went to bed, and to take my mind off my troubles I started to flick the pages of my beloved Cellini. The charm worked, as I read the snatches of his adventures of art and of Renaissance virility, his love for the goblets and the statues he made out of materials he adored, his imprisonments, his escapes, his dealings with his fellow goldsmiths and sculptors, his homicides and brawls, and again his delight in every aspect of his craft. Every page I turned was, to me, as it still is, sheer magic:

> . . . Sure, therefore, that I could trust them, I gave my attention to the furnace, which I had filled up with pigs of copper and pieces of bronze, laid one on top of the other, according to the rules of the craft—that is, not

pressing closely one on the other, but arranged so that the flames could make their way freely about them; for in this manner the metal is more quickly affected by the heat and liquefied. Then in great excitement I ordered them to light the furnace. They piled on the pine logs; and between the unctuous pine resin and the well-contrived draught of the furnace, the fire burned so splendidly that I had to feed it now on one side and now on the other. The effort was almost intolerable, yet I forced myself to keep it up.

On top of all this the shop took fire, and we feared lest the roof should fall upon us. Then, too . . .

I flicked over the pages, back and forth, reflecting how Cellini had enjoyed a long love affair with his art, how Cellini was comically contradictory in his actions, how boastful he was about his work.

. . . When I reached Piacenza, I met Duke Pier Luigi in the street, who stared me up and down, and recognised me. He had been the sole cause of all the wrong I had suffered in the castle of St. Angelo; and now I fumed at the sight of him. But not knowing any way of avoiding him, I made up my mind to go and pay him a visit. I arrived at the palace just as the table was being cleared. With him were some men of the house of Landi, those who were afterwards his murderers. When I came in, he received me with the utmost effusiveness; and among other pleasant things which

fell from his lips was his declaration to those
who were present that I was the greatest man
in all the world in my profession . . .

And so, forgetting my troubles, I flicked back to
the opening page, the opening paragraph of this
magnificent autobiography:

All men, whatever be their condition, who
have done anything of merit, or which verily
has a semblance of merit, if so be they are
men of truth and good repute, should write
the tale of their life with their own hand.

One day, I thought, I'll write the tale of my life.
But first I have to live.

. . . In truth it seems to me I have greater
content of mind and health of body than at
any time in the past. Some pleasant happen-
ings I recall, and, again, some unspeakable
misfortunes, which, when I remember, strike
terror into me and wonder that I have,
indeed, come to this age of fifty-eight, from
which, by God's grace, I am now going on my
way rejoicing.

The other day, while I was working on this
account of that small part of my life and all that
happened in the middle of the twentieth century,
those months of 1949–50, I read this last-quoted
passage and went back in my thoughts to the
spring of 1950 when I lay reading it in bed in my

room in Kensington. I was reflecting that one could take endless enchanting poems out of this book simply by flicking over the pages, back and forth, and extracting for oneself a page here, a paragraph there, and while I was playing with this idea it came to me with all apparent irrelevance that Dottie, who knew very well how my possessions were disposed in my room, had certainly taken my package that night the house-boy had let her in to wait for me.

It was after two in the morning. I jumped out of bed and put on my clothes. While dressing I remembered those proofs in Sir Quentin's desk and my curious passing notion that they were mine. Out I plunged into the cold night and trudged round to Dottie's. I don't know if it was raining, I noticed rain very little in those days. But I was cold, standing under her window singing "Auld Lang Syne." I was afraid of waking the neighbourhood but I was fairly enraged; I sang in as low a voice as I felt would penetrate Dottie's bedroom window, but persistently. A light went on in someone else's window, the sash went up and a head looked out. "Stop your bloody row at this time of night." I moved out of the light of the street-lamp and as I did so I saw the curtain in Dottie's room pulled aside. By the street-light I saw a head, not Dottie's, peering through the pane. It became apparent as I kept watch from the pavement that it was a man's head. I assumed it was Leslie. Dottie's outraged neighbour had withdrawn and slammed down the sash, and as the light went out in his window I saw more clearly, but only for a brief flash, that the head in Dottie's room was not Leslie's; it was a square face with a hairless head, and elderly; it seemed to me to be the face of Revisson Doe, my publisher.

I made quickly for home, convincing myself I had been mistaken. It is true I had *Warrender Chase* on my mind; it was altogether possible, considering the loss of my manuscript, that I had it on my brain.

Now Dottie, English Rose as she was, had always demonstrated herself to be a very pious, old-fashioned Catholic. I was convinced she had taken my *Warrender Chase,* but I still wasn't sure if she had done it as a half-joke or in one of her fits of righteousness; she was perfectly capable of burning a book she considered evil but I felt she would hardly go so far with my foolscap sheets. All my experience of Dottie was that she was basically harmless and, so far as she herself was conscious of sincerity, sincere. I wondered, too, if she had taken the novel to show to someone—some Carmelite divine to ask his no doubt adverse opinion of it, or Leslie, to curry favour with him by showing him the last part which he had never seen. I wondered everything. What I wondered most after I got home was who could be spending the night with Dottie. It wasn't her father, for I had met him. I thought perhaps it could be an elderly uncle. But back I came always to that glimpse I had got of the square face and bald head of Revisson Doe.

But it seemed impossible both that Dottie had a

lover and that Revisson Doe could, at his age, be one.

I sat up all that night bothering myself over these two apparent impossibilities. On the part of Dottie I saw lying on the table the evidence of a little folded card she had once left me, and which had turned up in the course of my search for my package. It was typical of Dottie. She had paid two shillings and sixpence to enrol me in something with this card. "Guild of Our Lady of Ransom" it was headed, going on to explain "for the Conversion of England. Jesus convert England. Under the Heavenly Patronage of *Our Lady, St. Gregory, and the Blessed English Martyrs.*" I sat and looked at this, drinking in Dottie's piety. "Motto:" it announced on the inside, "For God, Our Lady, and the Catholic Faith." This was followed by "Obligations. 1. To say the Daily Prayer for the Intentions of the Guild. 2. To work for the objects of the Guild. 3. To subscribe at least Two Shillings and Sixpence a year to the Ransom Fund. Fleur Talbot [in Dottie's handwriting] is hereby enrolled a Red Cross Ransomer. Partial Indulgences 1. *Seven Years and Seven Quarantines.* 2. *One Hundred Days.*"

And so it went on, with its bureaucratic Indulgences, its Souls in Purgatory and all the rest of Dottie's usual claptrap.

I too was a Catholic believer but not that sort, not that sort at all. And if it was true, as Dottie always said, that I was taking terrible risks with my immortal soul, I would have been incapable of caution on those grounds. I had an art to practise

128

and a life to live, and faith abounding; and I simply didn't have the time or the mentality for guilds and indulgences, fasts and feasts and observances. I've never held it right to create more difficulties in matters of religion than already exist.

I say this, because it struck me as strange that a man's head which was not Leslie's should appear at Dottie's bedroom window at two-thirty in the night. Again, as I pondered, I caught in my mind's eye the head of Revisson Doe. I had only seen him a few times. Could it be possible? I began to feel I had perhaps misjudged his age. I had thought him about sixty. In fact, I was sure he was about sixty. The impossible, as I thought on and on, became possible. I hadn't got an impression of a sexually active man, but then I hadn't really looked at him from that point of view. The possibility existed, except, of course, that Dottie would die rather than be unfaithful to a living husband; she would consider it a mortal sin, she would sink straight to hell if she were run over in the street unabsolved. I knew Dottie's way of thinking. It was impossible. And yet, as the birds of Kensington began to chirp in the early spring dawn outside my window, Dottie's infidelity piped up its entire possibility.

I thought it possible she had made a point of meeting Revisson Doe with a view to getting Leslie's novel published. It was possible she was immolating herself on the altar of Leslie's book. She was a pretty woman and it was possible that Revisson Doe, sixty or seventy as he might be, should go to bed with her. It was all unlikely but it was all quite possible. I concluded my due process of induction with the thought that it was not very unlikely, and really quite probable; and I was left with the fact I still didn't know for certain if Dottie had taken my *Warrender Chase,* and, if so, why. It was five in the morning. I set my alarm for eight and went to bed.

Chapter Eight

I got a letter by the first post in a Park and Revisson Doe Co. Ltd. envelope, which I opened bleary-eyed.

> Dear Fleur (if I may),
>
> A small problem has cropped up with regard to your novel *Warrender Chase*.
>
> I think we should talk this over face to face before proceeding further, as the details are too complicated to explain by letter.
>
> Please ring me at your earliest opportunity to make an appointment for us to meet, to think out this delicate matter.
>
> Always,
>
> Revisson

This letter appalled me. It is typical of a state of anxiety that it seems to attract ever more disaster. It was a quarter to nine. Park and Revisson Doe didn't start business till ten. I decided to ring at half-past ten. I read the letter over and over again, each time with greater foreboding. What was wrong with my *Warrender Chase?* I took the letter sentence by sentence; each one looked worse than the other. After half an hour I decided I had to talk to somebody. I had no intention of returning to the Hallam Street carnival. Even before the letter arrived I had made up my mind only to wander in later in the day, collect some things that I had left behind, say good-bye to Edwina and look for another job.

I made an appointment with Revisson Doe for three-thirty that day. I tried to pump him on the phone, whether there was "something wrong" with my *Warrender Chase* but he wouldn't be drawn into any discussion. He sounded edgy, rather unfriendly. He addressed me as Miss Talbot, forgetting about Fleur if he might. I didn't know then, as I know now, that the traditional paranoia of authors is as nothing compared to the inalienable schizophrenia of publishers.

Revisson Doe on the phone was plainly nervous about something, I supposed about the loss of money my book was likely to incur, I supposed he wanted to revise the terms of the contract, I supposed he might want me to change something vital in the novel and I decided throughout all this supposing that I would refuse to make any changes in the book. I wondered, then, if Theo and Audrey had expressed their adverse opinions on the book to my publisher when they had sent back the proofs. I had written a note to thank them for the proof-reading and had been inclined not to believe Dottie when she had reported with such ferocity what Theo and Audrey, always so good to me, had said. But that morning, sleepless, and with a terrible yesterday behind me, I was fairly at my wits' end. I rang up the Clairmont house; their maid answered and I asked for either Theo or Audrey. The maid came back to say they were both busy in their studies.

I went back to bed and by the afternoon felt ready for my interview with Revisson Doe. I was so far refreshed that I was able to rather look forward to the meeting, anxious to have another look at him from the point of view of his possibly being Dottie's or anyone else's bedfellow. I just had time on the way to stop at Kensington Public Library to look up his age in *Who's Who*. Born 1884. He had been married twice, one son, two daughters. I got on the bus calculating that he was sixty-six. It seemed older to me in those days than it does now. When I saw Revisson Doe there in his office, I was sure that his was the head I had seen at Dottie's window. I took the chair he waved me into, wondering if Dottie had told the old goat that it was probably I who had been singing "Auld Lang Syne" at two-thirty in the morning. But he gave no sign of embarrassment on that score. At the same time I thought, whatever Dottie saw in him it was not sex-appeal.

"Now," he said, "I want you to know that we value your work highly." I noticed the "we" and felt uneasy. At the time when he had been considering *Warrender Chase* he had dithered between "I" and "we" quite a lot. To express his enthusiasm and keenness for the book as a new young piece of writing he had used "I" both in his letters and conversations; to signify the risk of a loss on the deal he had always put it down to "we." Now we were back at "we" again.

"We understand you're working on a new novel?"

I said yes, it was to be entitled *All Souls' Day.*

He said it didn't sound a very selling title. "Of course," he said, "we can change the title."

I said that was to be the title.

"Oh, well, we have an option on it. We can discuss the title later. We were debating whether it wouldn't perhaps be preferable to leave *Warrender Chase* aside for the time being. You see a first novel is after all a pure experiment, isn't it? Whereas, we were going to suggest if you would let us see the opening chapters of the second novel, your *All Fools' Day*—"

"*All Souls' Day,*" I said.

"*All Souls' Day,* yes, oh, quite." He seemed to be amused at this, and I took advantage of his little laugh to ask him what was wrong with *Warrender Chase.*

"We can't publish it," he said.

"Why not?"

"Fortunately for us we've discovered in time that it bears the fault of most first novels, alas, it is too close to real life. Why, look, you know, these characters of yours are lifted clean from that Autobiographical Association you work for. We have, really we have, looked into the matter and we have a number of testimonies to the likeness. And now your employer, Sir Quentin Oliver, is threatening to sue. He asked us for a sight of the proofs and naturally we gave him a set. You make them out to be sinister, you make them out to be feeble, hypnotized creatures and you make Sir Quentin out to be an evil manipulator and hater of women. He drives one woman to suicide and another—"

"My novel was started before I met Sir Quentin Oliver. The man must be mad."

"He's threatening to sue if we publish. Sir Quentin Oliver is a man of substance. We can't afford to risk a libel suit. The very idea . . ." He put his hand over his eyes for a moment. Then he said, "It's out of the question. But we do value your potentialities as a writer very highly, Miss Talbot—Fleur, if I may—and if we could offer you some guidance with your second novel from our fund of experience, it may be possible to switch the contract—"

"I don't need your guidance."

"You would be the first author I've known who could not, between ourselves, do with a little editorial help. You must remember," said he, for all the world as if I were incapable of disgust, "that an author is a publisher's raw material."

I said I would have to consult my advisers and got up to leave. "We are very unhappy about this, most unhappy," he said. I never saw him again.

It wasn't till after I got home that I realized he had my only copy of the typescript of *Warrender Chase*. I didn't want to ask for it back until I had consulted Solly Mendelsohn, lest I should jeopardize the contract; I half hoped that Solly would

135

suggest some way in which they could be induced to change their minds; but at the same time I knew I couldn't deal any more with Park and Revisson Doe. The shock and disappointment had been too sudden for me to plunge into the final reality of taking the physical book away from them. But I did, when I got home, ring up Revisson Doe. I got his secretary. He was engaged, could she help me? I said I would be obliged if she could send me a spare set of proofs as I had mislaid my original manuscript and I wanted to look through my *Warrender Chase*. "Hold on, please," she said politely and went off the line, I presumed for further instructions, for some minutes. She came back and said, "I'm so sorry, but the type has been distributed."

Ignorant as I was then of printers' jargon I said, "Distributed to whom?"

"Distributed—broken up. We are not printing the book, Miss Talbot."

"And what happened to the proofs?"

"Oh, those have been destroyed, naturally."

"Thank you."

I was able to get Solly on the phone at his office the next night. He told me to meet him at a pub in Fleet Street, and came down from his office for a quick conference.

"It's not them sue you for libel," Solly mused, "it's you sue them for saying your book's libellous. That's if they put it in writing. But it would cost you a fortune. Better get your typescript back and

136

tell them to wipe their arse with the contract. Don't give them your next novel. Don't worry. We'll get another publisher. But get the typescript back. It's yours by rights. By legal rights. You're a bloody fool not to have kept a copy."

"Well, I had the original manuscript. How could I know that Dottie, or whoever it was, would steal it?"

"I would say," said Solly, "that is was Dottie, all right. She's been acting like a fool over your novel. However, it's a good sign when people act like fools over a piece of work, a good sign."

I couldn't see how it was a good sign. I got home just before ten. I made plans to retrieve my typescript from the publisher the next day and also to make it my business to get back my manuscript from Dottie. The possibility that all copies of my *Warrender Chase* had been destroyed was one I couldn't face clearly that night, but it hung around me nightmarishly—the possibility that nowhere, nowhere in the world, did my *Warrender Chase* exist any more.

Then the telephone rang. It was Lady Edwina's nurse.

"I've been trying to get you all afternoon," she said. "Lady Edwina's asking for you. We've had a terrible time all day. Mrs. Tims and Sir Quentin were called out early this morning because his poor friend Lady Bernice Gilbert passed away. Then they came back and asked for you. Then they went out again. Lady Edwina's been laughing her head off. Hysterics. She's just dropping off now. I gave her a dose. But she wants to see you as soon—"

"What did Lady Bernice die of?"

"I'm afraid," said the nurse with a quivering voice, "she took her own life."

Chapter Nine

There and then the determination took me that, whatever Sir Quentin was up to, for myself, I was not any sort of victim; I was simply not constituted for the role. The news of Bernice Gilbert's suicide horrified but toughened me.

I went along to Hallam Street next morning. I felt sure, now, that not only was Sir Quentin exerting his influence to suppress my *Warrender Chase* but he was using, stealing, my myth. Without a mythology, a novel is nothing. The true novelist, one who understands the work as a continuous poem, is a myth-maker, and the wonder of the art resides in the endless different ways of telling a story, and the methods are mythological by nature.

I was sure, and it turned out that I was right, that Dottie had obtained for Sir Quentin a set of the proofs of *Warrender Chase* to read. I had been too free with that novel, I should never have made it known to Dottie in the first place. Never since have I shown my work to my friends or read it aloud to them before it has been published. However, it was our general custom at that time to read our work to each other, or send it to be read, and to discuss our

139

work with each other; that was literary life as I then knew it.

At the flat in Hallam Street Mrs. Tims was dabbing the corners of her eyes with a white handkerchief. "Where were you yesterday? Just when we needed you," she said. "Sir Quentin was most distressed."

"Where is he?"

She was startled by my tone. "He had to go out. The inquest is this afternoon. The poor—"

But I had gone into his study, shutting the door with a firm, sharp click. I went straight to the drawer where I had seen the proofs. The drawer was empty except for a set of keys. The other drawers were locked.

I went next to Edwina's room. She was sitting up in bed with her breakfast tray. The nurse was in Edwina's bathroom which led off from the bedroom, washing something. She put her head round the door.

Edwina was in a rational state, for her. She said, "Suicide. Just like the woman in your novel."

"I know."

I sat on the edge of her bed and telephoned to Park and Revisson Doe to ask them to send me the typescript of my *Warrender Chase*.

"Hold on, please." The girl was away for some long minutes during which I told Edwina that my book wasn't going to be published.

"Oh yes it is," said Edwina, "I shall see to it. My friend—" The secretary had come back on the phone. "I'm afraid the copy we had has been destroyed. Mr. Doe put it on his desk for you to take, and you didn't take it away. He thought you didn't want it."

"I didn't see it on his desk. I'm sure it wasn't there."

"Well Mr. Doe says he had it out for you. He says he threw it out. We haven't room to store manuscripts, Miss Talbot. Mr. Doe says we take no responsibility for the manuscripts. It is stated in the contract."

"Tell Mr. Doe I'll see my lawyer."

"That's right," said Edwina, when I had hung up, "tell them you'll see your lawyer."

"I haven't got a lawyer. And it would be no use."

"But you've given them something to think about," Edwina said. She had buttered a piece of crisp toast from her breakfast tray, and handed it to me. I munched it, thinking how I could go about writing *Warrender Chase* all over again. But I knew I couldn't. Something spontaneous had gone for ever if it were true that all the copies were destroyed including the proofs Sir Quentin had got hold of. I didn't tell Edwina that Sir Quentin had been the cause of my losing my publisher; on the whole, the old lady bore very well the fact that she had spawned a rotter; it wouldn't have done to rub it in. I thought of Edwina's courageous facing of facts again, later on, when she sat in her wheelchair in her pearls and black satin, quiet but fully alive, at Sir Quentin's funeral.

It did me good to sit on Edwina's bed that morning, eating the toast that she continued to butter and jam for me, with those ancient star-spangled banners, her long bejewelled hands, fluttering among the small porcelain dishes.

Beryl Tims came in once "to see if everything was all right." The nurse, a kindly soul called Miss Fisher, came out of the bathroom to assure her on this point. Edwina glared at Beryl Tims. I went on munching.

"I think," said Miss Fisher, "a fresh pot of tea might be called for and an extra cup."

"Oh, Fleur can come to the kitchen and have her morning coffee with mc."

"Nurse said tea," said Edwina. "We want it brought in here."

"Fleur has her work to do. We wouldn't want to keep Fleur back from her work, would we?" said the English Rose. "And you know that Miss Fisher didn't get her afternoon off yesterday. We're hoping Fleur will hold the fort this afternoon, aren't we? I shall be at the inquest with Sir Quentin this afternoon. So you and Fleur can have your tea together, can't you?"

Not a word of this was addressed to me, but I had a plan in mind which made this opportunity of spending some hours in the flat with no one except Edwina an exciting prospect. When Miss Fisher said, "Oh I wouldn't dream of leaving Lady Edwina at a time like this," I quickly put in that I'd be delighted to make afternoon tea and generally look after Lady Edwina.

"Miss Fisher needs a rest," said Beryl Tims.

"I quite agree with Mrs. Tims," I said, and

probably it was the first and only time I ever said such a thing.

So it was agreed. Miss Fisher with a bowl of washing followed Mrs. Tims out of the room. I got on the phone, now, to Solly Mendelsohn.

I didn't like phoning Solly during the day, for he slept most of the morning after his long night-duty. I always supposed, too, that he had some other private life, a woman we never met but who occupied his spare time; it wasn't the sort of thing one would want to find out and there was always something about Solly into which no real friend of his could intrude. But at least I knew he wouldn't have the phone off the hook in case of a call from the news-room at his paper, and in the emergency of the occasion I chanced it. He answered, half asleep. But when he heard my urgent voice making of him a few brief requests, Solly agreed to do exactly what I asked without further explanations.

Solly arrived at a quarter to four at Hallam Street, big, hulky and unshaven, wrapped in scarves. He looked very much like a burglar with his big, brown travelling bag. Edwina was sitting up in her chair in the drawing-room.

Sir Quentin had not returned to the flat; he was to meet Beryl Tims at the Coroner's Inquest on Bernice Gilbert's suicide while of unsound mind. But as soon as Beryl Tims had left I had made a good snoop around Sir Quentin's study. The proofs of *Warrender Chase* were nowhere to be found. But the keys in the unlocked drawer of his desk opened the cabinet wherein, as Sir Quentin always said, "were secrets."

One after the other of the drawers contained the files, Sir Quentin's notes of the members of the Autobiographical Association. Mrs. Wilks was there, the Baronne Clotilde du Loiret, Miss Maisie Young, Father Egbert Delaney, Sir Eric Findlay and the late Bernice "Bucks" Gilbert, widow of the former chargé d'affaires in San Salvador, Sir Alfred Gilbert. . . . These were the files I was interested in. There was a file marked "Beryl, Mrs. Tims," which I ignored. I had decided to take these files as hostages for my *Warrender Chase*, which I was perfectly sure Sir Quentin had arranged with Dottie to steal from my room.

But as I had waited for Solly's arrival I had also flicked through one of the memoirs, for I was curious to see what had been added under Sir Quentin's management since he had taken them out of my hands. And I had time enough to see, as I turned over one file after another, that, although nothing had been added in the form of memoirs, sheets of notes, some typed, some in Sir Quentin's hand, had been inserted, familiar passages; they were lifted more or less directly from my *Warrender Chase*.

I closed the cabinet again with its secrets when Solly rang the door-bell. Edwina, dressed in her full regalia, exclaimed her joy to see him. I sat him down beside her, rather bewildered as he was, and I explained to them both: "I'm going to take away

144

the memoirs of the Autobiographical Association to work on at home. Those biographies do need a literary touch."

Solly seemed to begin to understand. Edwina uncannily seemed to perceive something that even I did not, for she said, "What a splendid idea! That will save more of these tragedies. Poor Bucks Gilbert!"

I told Solly, then, that Lady Bernice had committed suicide, and that the inquest was proceeding at that moment. And I took his bag leaving him with Edwina.

I put the files in Solly's bag. It was an exhilarating affair. I thought how easy it was to steal, and I thought of Sir Quentin stealing my book, not only the physical copies, but the very words, phrases, ideas. Even from the brief look I had taken I could see he had even stolen a letter I had invented, written from my Warrender Chase to my character Marjorie. The bag was heavy. I lugged it into the hall and put it by the front door.

When I got back to the drawing-room, Solly had lit the pretty silver spirit-stove under the kettle which Edwina liked to use for her afternoon tea. It was a bit early for tea-time but Edwina was always "weary for tea" as she put it. There were some buttered scones, some biscuits, which Solly had already started to help himself to. Edwina said, "Where are the files? Have you put them in that bag?"

I said I had. I said Sir Quentin would not miss

them right away, no doubt, but he would realize I was really in better condition working on them at home.

"Take them away, darling," shrieked Edwina. Then she came out with, "You'll never get your novel back if you don't do something about it."

Solly then said to me, "Haven't you managed to find a copy?"

"No," I said, "the whole book's disappeared."

"I knew it," said Edwina. "Somehow I knew it. They think I don't know what's going on in this house because I'm asleep most of the time. But I'm not asleep."

She went on to list the names of the publishers she knew personally whom she could get to publish my book should she but crook her little finger. Some of them, it is true, had been dead half a century. But we let that go and made ourselves very optimistic over our tea.

Sir Quentin and Mrs. Tims came in rather earlier than I had expected, before Solly left.

"To whom," said Sir Quentin as he came into the room, "does that bag in the hall belong?"

"It's mine," said Solly, getting up.

"Baron von Mendelsohn," I said, "is only passing through. May I introduce, Sir Quentin Oliver—the Baron von—"

"Oh, please, please, dear Baron, do sit down. . . ." Sir Quentin in his usual orgasm over a title, fussed round unshaven Solly, begging him to sit down, to stay, not to leave.

But Solly, solid and unshaken by his new-found

title said polite good-byes all round and limped off, staggering a little at the door under the unexpected weight of the bag.

"Suicide while of unsound mind," said Sir Quentin when he came back into the room. "An overdose of sleeping pills knocked back by a pint of whisky. I really must see that something more seemly goes on the death certificate."

"Tell them," yelled Edwina, "to wipe their arse with the death certificate."

"Mummy!"

I left shortly afterwards, and took an expensive taxi home to catch up with Solly.

Chapter Ten

It is not to be supposed that the stamp and feeling of a novel can be conveyed by an intellectual summary. My references to the book have been scrappy: I couldn't reproduce my *Warrender Chase* in a few words; and anyhow, an attempt to save, or not save, anyone the trouble of reading it would be simply beside the point.

But I can certainly meet my essential purpose, which is to tell how Sir Quentin Oliver tried to arrange for the destruction of *Warrender Chase* as a novel at the same time as he appropriated the spirit of my legend for his own use. I can show how he actually plagiarized my text. And so I am writing about the cause of an effect.

I remember as a young child being obliged to write out in my copy-book, Necessity is the Mother of Invention. The sample had already been effected in beautiful copperplate on the first line, and to improve our handwriting it was our task to copy out this maxim on the lines below, which I duly did, all unaware that I was not merely acquiring an improved calligraphy but imbibing at the same time a subliminal lesson in social ethics. Another maxim was All is not Gold that Glisters, and another was Honesty is the Best Policy, and I also recall Discretion is the Better Part of Valour. And I have to testify that these precepts, which I was too flighty-minded to actually ponder at the time, but around which I dutifully curled my cursive Ps and my Vs, have turned out to my astonishment to be absolutely true. They may lack the grandeur of the Ten Commandments but they are more to the point.

Necessity, therefore, being the mother of invention, it was not surprising that the first thing I did after Solly had left me with the heavy bag of troubles I had taken from Hallam Street was to ring up a number of friends and alert them that I was now looking for another job.

When these seeds had been sown I heaved the bag of biographies into the bottom of my clothes cupboard for the time being. I started to lay plans for the retrievement of my stolen manuscript of *Warrender Chase*. I was tempted to ring up Dottie and confront her with the theft. Discretion is the better part of valour; with difficulty I restrained myself. I felt she wasn't quite the same Dottie with whom I had been basically friendly with an occasional blazing row. Something had happened to change her; almost certainly Sir Quentin's influence. I had torn up her biography; I hoped she had taken my advice and refused to take further part in memoir-writing for Sir Quentin.

I began to brood on the outrages perpetrated upon me and my novel by Dottie, Sir Quentin,

Revisson Doe; I tried to imagine the justifications they could have variously produced: that I was mad, the book was mad, it was evil, it was libellous, it ought to be suppressed. There came to my mind a phrase of John Henry Newman's in his journals: ". . . the thousand whisperings against me . . ." No sooner had I thought of this than I decided to put an end to my brooding. Finish. Cut it out.

In the meantime as often happens when I brood, a plan of action had been forming in my mind. I didn't think Dottie would be so far gone under Sir Quentin's hypnotic influence as to have destroyed my book, but I wasn't prepared to take the risk of alarming her to the extent that she might have time to do so. I determined somehow or other to retrieve my *Warrender Chase* by stealth. For which I would need to get the key of Dottie's flat and I would need to get her out of her flat for some hours without fear of her returning. Furthermore I would have to be sure that Leslie shouldn't burst in on me while I was searching the flat. I felt quite excited. It was like writing the pages of a novel, and I consciously kept these plans fixed in part of my brain to transform into the last chapters of *All Souls' Day,* as I eventually did in my own shadowy way. People often ask me where I get ideas for my novels; I can only say that my life is like that, it turns into some other experience of fiction, recognizable only to myself. And part of my indignation at having been accused of libelling the Auto-biographical Association in my *Warrender Chase* was this: that even if I had invented the characters after, not before, I had gone to work at Sir Quentin's—even if I had been moved to portray those poor people in fictional form, they would not have been recognizable, even to themselves—even in that case, there would have been no question of libel. Such as I am, I'm an artist, not a reporter.

To return to my plan. I needed an accomplice, maybe two. I needed the sort of accomplices who were either completely faithful to the idea that what I was doing was legitimate, or else were not entirely aware of what my plan consisted of.

I wondered, first, if I could somehow wheedle the key to the flat out of Leslie. I could have done so, I think. I'm sure my sexual attraction for Leslie alone would have been strong enough to have brought off some design of that kind. It would have taken time, it would have taken an effort on my part. It was the effort that finally put me right off the idea. Not that I couldn't imagine, in the situation I could have arranged, finding Leslie quite possible to go to bed with, for he really had a great deal of masculine charm. I could see that I could ask him to come round with a book that I needed, as in past times I used so often to do; I could say I needed some help with a passage in Newman, as I did so often in the past when I needed a reference book for those long, devoted, underpaid but often well-appreciated articles I wrote for church newspapers and literary magazines, so making myself into a wayside authority on

Newman that I always got Newman books to write about. But the fact that I couldn't just ask Leslie for a loan of the key—that I couldn't trust him merely with my story, and engage him on my side—put me quite off the idea. Absolutely I would have had to go to bed with him again, work up to the old intimacy, before I could confide, or half-confide, my predicament. Nothing doing, I thought. Even though it would have been the natural thing to let him stay the night if I were going to spend an evening with him, nothing doing. I let his handsome young face recede from my thoughts, far handsomer than Wally McConnachie's. Wally's face was big-boned and Wally was built on the heavy side, not quite squat but nothing like so lithe as Leslie. However, Wally's face took shape in my mind's eye as Leslie's receded. I was growing rather fond of Wally.

Now another reflection took hold of me: It is strange how one knows one's friends more clearly as one sees them imaginatively in various situations. The moment I thought of Wally—how it should be if I were to tell him about my *Warrender Chase*, how Dottie (whom he didn't know) had said it was mad, how Theo and Audrey Clairmont (whom he knew) had behaved so oddly, how my publisher had cancelled the contract on an unverified suspicion of libel—if I should tell Wally all this story, and the story of Sir Quentin's plagiarizing my novel, and the story of Dottie's probably stealing my novel, and how I had stolen the biographies—it seemed unfeasible that I should tell Wally all that. One item, perhaps, but not the lot. I ruled Wally out because I knew instinctively how he would react. I could imagine my saying, "And Wally, you know, Bernice Gilbert's suicide is so like the suicide of a character in my novel." And Wally would say, "Look Fleur, this is all a bit fantastic you know. Poor Bucks Gilbert has always been a bit, well . . ." And all the time would be working at the back of his mind a word to himself, in relation to his own life, his job, his place in society, a word of caution: Don't get mixed up in this, Wally. He would say to himself, These authors, these bohemians. He would say to me, "I'd let it rest, Fleur, I really would. I daresay your manuscript will turn up."

Or suppose I said (as I thought it possible I might), "Wally, please will you take my friend Dottie to the theatre? I'll arrange it. I want to go and search her flat for my novel." Then Wally would probably say, "I wouldn't take that risk if I were you, Fleur dear," meaning, I don't want to take the risk of being implicated myself . . . a scandal . . .

I can never know how it would have gone in reality. But in reality I didn't apply to Wally for help. Wally was a love, and I wanted to keep him for the fun that we had and might have together. It involved keeping him in that compartment of life in which it had pleased God to place him, set apart from my present most mysterious, slightly hallucinatory concerns.

154

Wally rang me just as I had come to this point in my reflections. He had "just got away," was I doing anything? "Just got away" was one of Wally's frequent phrases, it might have been from his office, from a party; I never asked him, but I've noticed throughout my life that Foreign Office people are generally wont to put in their appearance with the words, I've just got away; one dares not ask from where, it might be Top Secret. Anyway, I said no, I wasn't doing anything, no, I hadn't dined, I had barely touched my tea. It was agreed between us that it was a brilliant idea for me to be ready in half an hour, he would pick me up and we would go to eat in Soho. Wasn't it awful, he said before he hung up, about Bucks Gilbert?

I said it was ghastly.

Before I left I locked the door of my clothes cupboard and took the key.

Wally spoke of Bucks Gilbert at dinner.

"Had you seen her since her party?"

"Only once, very briefly, the same day that she died. She came to Hallam Street. She looked a bit upset."

"What about?" said Wally.

"Oh, I don't know, I don't know at all."

"I feel rather guilty," said Wally. "I suppose everyone does when a friend takes their life. One feels one could have done more. One could have done something if only one had known."

"Well, you didn't know."

"I could have known. She rang me up and left a message. It was a few days after the party. A fellow in the office took the message, I was to ring her back. He said she sounded awfully frantic. That rather put me off, I'm afraid. I wasn't really up to coping. Bucks was a clinging sort of woman you know, she used to cling. I wasn't up to it."

"Maybe someone was getting her down."

"That's what I've been wondering—what makes you say that?"

"An intuition. I'm a novelist, you know."

"Well you may be right," he said. "Because she rang up some other friends in those days after the party. Three people that I know of. Naturally, they're shattered. In each case they either didn't ring back or made an excuse."

"Were they people who were at the party?" I said.

He thought for a moment. "Yes," he said then, "they were. Why d'you ask that?"

"Maybe she was putting them to the test, to see if she really had any friends. Maybe that's why she gave the party. Someone could have put her up to it, to undermine her, convincing her she had no real friends."

"Oh, God, Fleur, I say, now you really are romancing. Oh, God, I hope it isn't true. I only went to the party because, well, one does look in on a cocktail party. If one can get away. Oh, God, surely she wasn't putting me to a test."

I was sorry for Wally. I regretted having spoken my thoughts. I was thinking of the Greek girl who committed suicide in my *Warrender Chase*. But I said that, obviously, Bernice Gilbert had some

156

private mental anxiety. "Nobody can help such people, nobody," I said. "The verdict was suicide while of unsound mind, Wally," I said. "Like most suicides. One can't do a thing about them, Wally."

"I wondered, in fact," Wally went on, "how she was able to lay on such a sumptuous reception, it really was rather grand, wasn't it? She wasn't a bit well-off you know. Half of the stuff must have come off the black market. There must have been three hundred people, you remember more were arriving when we left." Then Wally immediately pulled himself together, and smiled at me. He leant over the table and took my hand. "We mustn't get morbid. Let's snap out of it," he said. "After all, it was at poor Bucks's party that we got together, wasn't it?"

"Yes, that's true."

"So I can't regret having gone."

I told Wally I was leaving my job, looking for another.

"That calls for a drink. Will you come back to Ebury Street for a drink?"

I said I wasn't really up to a late night. I meant all night.

"Well we can go to the Gargoyle. What about the Gargoyle?"

I hesitated. Then I said yes, but first I'd have to go home and get something. Wally agreed, making so little of it that I supposed he thought it was my monthly period. In reality I wanted to look in at my room to see that the bag of biographies in my hanging-cupboard was still there. It would have been easy for Dottie to coax her way into my room. She had already got into the good favour of the house-boy by giving him holy pictures of the Little Flower. I knew Sir Quentin would soon discover the loss of the biographies.

Wally waited in the taxi while I dashed indoors.

My room was as usual. Nothing had been touched. The biographies were still there. I felt foolish for my nerviness. I locked the cupboard again and was leaving the room when the house-boy appeared before me. Yes, indeed Dottie had been round to see me.

"Did she wait in my room?"

"No, Miss. Yourself told me the last time the lady was here for you that nobody was to be let in your room again."

"Oh, thanks very much, Harry. I forgot I'd told you. It was quite right of you. Thanks very much." I gave him two shillings to ease the affront, which amazed him. As I ran out to the taxi, I thought again how nervy I was becoming. After the loss of my *Warrender Chase* I had told not only Harry, but the maid and the landlord, very firmly that no one should be allowed into my room while I wasn't there. I decided to suppress my nerves and take courage.

We went to the Gargoyle. I had a crème de menthe, Wally a whisky. There were three groups of people, none of whom we knew, and one wispy young man all alone in a shadowy corner with a drink in front of him. I looked at him again; it was Gray Mauser.

158

"The boy in the corner," I said to Wally, "is called Gray Mauser."

This cheered Wally immensely.

"He writes under the name of Leander. He's a poet." As I spoke Gray looked over to me and I gave him a little wave.

"Would you like him to join us?" said Wally.

"Yes, I would."

Gray set in immediately to make eyes at Wally, and he flicked his weak little wrists around, and wriggled somewhat. Wally took this in good part.

"My friend," Gray said, "has gone to Ireland for three weeks." He sat so that he was three-quarters facing Wally with the same amount of his back to me. Wally shifted quietly so that Gray had to face us both. "He gave me this tie, my friend. Do you like it?"

"Very effective," said Wally, and went on talking affably, so arranging things that Gray was forced to give a little attention to me. Gray was totally unaware of these manoeuvres, for he was genuinely well-meaning but at the same time overwhelmingly taken with Wally.

But when I got Gray's attention I took advantage of the moment to say right out, "Gray, I wonder if Leslie took the key of Dottie's flat to Ireland with him?"

"No darling," said Gray. "It's on our dressing-table at this moment, right where he left it. Why?"

So I explained to them both how I needed to borrow that key, as a secret, because I wanted to go to Dottie's flat to leave a surprise for her. I explained to Wally that Gray's friend was an old friend of mine whose wife, Dottie, was also a friend of mine. By the time we had finished our drinks, and Wally and I had made simultaneous "Let's-go" signs to each other, Gray had promised to lend me the key and keep it ever such a secret. I was to pick up the key the following afternoon.

I fell asleep that night while I was still trying to think of people I could induce to take Dottie to the theatre. I thought of Solly. He had two nights off a week. My dear Solly, he was always so good, I didn't want to become a weight on him. He probably wanted his two nights to himself. Besides he was a poet, and a real one. Then I remembered something that made me exclude Solly, anyway. Dottie disliked him. She would hardly be persuaded to go to the theatre with Solly. I remembered on the two occasions she had met Solly she had asked me afterwards what I saw in him. I thought this strange because everybody else I knew, including Leslie, loved Solly. She had said she thought Solly attractive but vulgar. Solly had not given her the slightest provocation for thinking so. He always kept his invectives and profanities for his nearest and trusted friends and had said nothing Dottie could take exception to. I said he was the least vulgar-spirited of men. "Oh," said Dottie, "I don't mean spiritual vulgarity." "What other sort of vulgarity can there be?" I said, which was perhaps arguable. But Dottie had left it at that, since she evidently felt I might win the argument, if by word only.

So I dropped off to sleep musing on the fact that Solly wasn't at all vulgar in the same sense that Dottie was. Dottie, the English Rose.

I woke next morning knowing exactly what to do. I had twice decided not to return to Hallam Street, and now for the second time I was obliged to go back.

I wanted to get to Edwina. It was unlikely that I should get through to her on the telephone. Always, when I phoned her in my private time, Beryl Tims or Sir Quentin would make some excuse, usually that she was sleeping or not very well. If she herself wanted to get in touch with me at week-ends it was easy. She had a phone at her bedside, or sometimes the nurse would convey a message.

Now I wanted to see Edwina. I had a good excuse, too, for calling at Hallam Street, for I could then hand in a proper letter of resignation and collect my pay, my health card with the stamps that papered its folding walls as in a dolls' house, and other bureaucratic evidence of my reality, like my pay-as-you-earn tax paper, all of which I had intended to arrange by post, before I woke up with my certainty that I had to see Edwina.

It was a rainy morning, rather cold, and a Saturday.

"Sir Quentin has left for his property in North-umberland," Beryl Tims announced when I ar-

161

rived about ten o'clock. Sir Quentin always referred to people's houses in the country or abroad as their property. "He left by car at eight-thirty," she added, pompously.

"Where did he get the petrol?" I said sharply. Petrol was still rationed; it would not be off the ration till later in the month, the twenty-sixth to be precise; I remember the date because I had promised Wally to go down for the week-end of the twenty-seventh–twenty-eighth to his cottage at Marlow in his car, to celebrate the end of petrol-rationing. But the petrol-rationing laws still in force were very strict; some prominent people had gone to prison for transgressing them. So my question "Where did he get the petrol?" was a nasty little question, containing a menace of that citizens' righteousness which was quite rife in those days among ill-natured or grievance-burdened people. Beryl Tims was flustered. "I'm sure, I'm quite positive," said she, "that Sir Quentin has Supplementary. He would have to do, I mean, wouldn't he, for his poor mother?"

"Oh, has he taken Lady Edwina?"

"No, she's having her breakfast."

"Then he shouldn't be using her petrol coupons, should he?" I said. "We'll have to look into this," I went on in a voice which fairly took even myself aback. "Is his journey really necessary? We'll see." I walked past Beryl to the study door. The door, the stable-door, was locked.

"Sir Quentin," said the English Rose—she was

wearing a shocking-pink twin set she had got for Easter—"has left instructions that you are not, definitely, to enter the study. Sir Quentin, I believe, has written you a letter of dismissal. He has appointed a certain new lady assistant to commence on Monday."

"Well, I'll see Lady Edwina," I said, starting down the corridor that led to her room.

Beryl followed me. "Sir Quentin told me that if you phoned or called I was to ask you to return immediately the work that you took home with you. It should not have left this house."

I got to Edwina's door. Beryl clutched my arm. "You may," said Beryl, "see Lady Edwina. You may even," she said, "take her out tomorrow so that Nurse Fisher can get away. Lady Edwina's fluxive precipitations have augmented in frequency, and it is only because of the doctor's orders that she's to be spared distress and excitement that you are to be permitted the privilege of seeing her on the condition that she knows nothing of any dispute between yourself and Sir—"

The nurse opened the door just then. "Oh, good morning, Fleur," she said, while Edwina squealed from her bed, "Come and have some tea and toast. Tims—a fresh pot, please, and another cup."

"It's a quarter past ten," said Beryl.

"A fresh pot of tea, and step on the gas," yelled Edwina.

"I'll come and get it," said Miss Fisher.

When I sat on Edwina's bed she buttered a piece

163

of toast for me and said softly, with many a wild grimace, "He's got a new secretary."

"Is it Dottie?"

"Yes, of course. Ha-ha. He got Tims to burn some proofs of a book. She flushed the ashes down the lavatory. What a mess, all black."

I put my head close to hers and mouthed some words very clearly and carefully. I said, "Listen, Edwina, I want you to take this in. I want to have Dottie out of the way for three hours tomorrow afternoon. I will say I can't possibly manage to take you out tomorrow. If Miss Fisher offers to give up her afternoon-off, you are to refuse the offer. You are to demand Dottie. Make a fuss till you get Dottie to come. Be sure to keep her with you for at least three hours."

The old woman's eyes gleamed, her mouth made a great O, her head nodded in time to the rhythm of my phrases. She was taking it in.

"While Dottie is with you, take ill. Make her ring up the doctor. If he's out make her get another doctor. Wet your knickers twenty times. At all costs, get Dottie to stay with you and keep her with you."

She nodded.

"Three hours."

"Three hours," said Edwina.

I rang the bell of Dottie's flat when I went there the next day with a shopping bag in my hand, at two in the afternoon, just in case someone should

164

be there. No answer. I let myself in with the key. I locked myself in.

"Accused was familiar with the flat," I thought to myself as I went straight into the bathroom in a state of suspicious dread to look for signs of black paper-ash in the lavatory pan. I found no signs. I went into the bedroom, took off my coat and put it on the bed with my shopping bag. I had brought with me in the bag a small present, wrapped in pink tissue paper, a hand-embroidered silk hand-kerchief-case which I had never used, and which befitted an English Rose more than it did the likes of me. I intended to produce it as an alibi should I be caught in the flat.

I made for Dottie's desk in her bedroom. There was a page in her typewriter; Dottie was evidently making a fair copy of a much-corrected typescript in an open folder on the desk. I would have liked to linger over it, for it was evidently Leslie's novel; I glanced quickly at the cover of the folder to verify this and passed quickly to my main objective. *Warrender Chase* was nowhere on the desk. Nor was it in the drawers, in one of which, however, I came across a letter dated three weeks back, headed Park and Revisson Doe. It began "Dear Dottie (if I may) . . ." I didn't stop to read on but a super-stitious impulse caused me to drag my coat and shopping bag off the bed lest they should be contaminated. I left my things on the floor and continued my search of the bedroom. In the cupboards, on top of the cupboards, under the pillows, the mattress. Under the bed was a suitcase. I dragged it out. It was full of Dottie's summer clothes. No *Warrender Chase* anywhere. There remained the sitting-room, a spare bedroom which had also been Leslie's study, the kitchen and the linen cupboard in the bathroom. I disposed of the linen cupboard; nothing there. I felt that the probabilities were in favour of Leslie's study so I left it to the last. I started to ransack the sitting-room, lifting the cushions off the sofa and chairs and putting them back, searching behind the curtains and under piles of magazines. Nearly an hour had passed, and with the familiarity of the objects I touched and under which I peered came the doubt whether Dottie—exasperating but familiar old Dottie—had taken the manuscript at all.

I had finished with the sitting-room; everything was in place. I went out to the little hall to go into Leslie's work-room, the door of which was wide open showing the masses of untidy papers and shelves of books that I knew from old times. I think I even got as far as to look round the room. But as I had passed through the door I had seen underneath the coats which were hanging on two pegs by the door Dottie's black bag with her knitting, the red scarf protruding. I turned back to it. The notion came to me that I should examine this; no doubt Dottie had brought her knitting with her the night she had waited in my room and— But already my fingers had found a package, the size of a London telephone directory, wedged at the

166

bottom of the ghastly black bag. Out I whisked that package in a flash, and in another flash had opened it. My *Warrender Chase*, my novel, my Warrender, Warrender Chase; my foolscap pages with the first chapters I had once torn up, and then stuck together; my *Warrender Chase, mine.* I hugged it. I kissed it. I went to Dottie's bedroom and put it in my own shopping bag. I snatched from Dottie's desk an unopened ream of typing paper. This I wedged at the bottom of Dottie's bag, and carefully arranged the knitting on top of it. I put on my coat, took my shopping bag on my arm, looked carefully round the flat to see if everything was in place. I straightened the covers on the revolting bed, let myself out of the flat and went on my way rejoicing.

I have never known an artist who at some time in his life has not come into conflict with pure evil, realized as it may have been under the form of disease, injustice, fear, oppression or any other ill element that can afflict living creatures. The reverse doesn't hold: that is to say, it isn't only the artist who suffers, or who perceives evil. But I think it true that no artist has lived who has not experienced and then recognized something at first too incredibly evil to seem real, then so undoubtedly real as to be undoubtedly true. I was dying to look into the Pandora's box of Sir Quentin's biographies. But I had first to set about making typed copies of my *Warrender Chase,* it was

167

imperative; for I was determined not to let the work out of my hands until I had spare copies to send to a publisher. I started this business as soon as I got home that Sunday afternoon. I recall that I stopped only to ring Solly.

"I got my manuscript back," I told him. "All the proofs and the typescripts were destroyed." I then described my raid on Dottie's flat.

I gave him a full account. He was very solemn. He let loose a number of ill wishes upon the heads of Revisson Doe, Dottie and Sir Quentin Oliver. Then he said he would get me a new publisher if it was the last thing he did. Solly had always believed in the value of *Warrender Chase*. For myself, I felt towards it only that it was mine, my own, mine, and I still felt my novel *All Souls' Day,* which I had started, was far superior.

"Let me know when you've got the novel ready for a publisher," Solly said.

So I went on typing *Warrender Chase.* I had very few corrections to make, it was simple slog work. I stopped only to ring Hallam Street to enquire how Edwina was.

"She has had a bad day," said Mrs. Tims. "I can't stop now, good-bye." And she put down the phone. I had a whisky and soda and ate a poached egg, then I continued my labours. At midnight I was still typing. Every now and then I had to wash my hands because the two carbon sheets—I had determined to make three typed sets of the novel in all—were constantly blackening them. At mid-

night more or less, Dottie started singing "Auld
Lang Syne" outside my window. I thought her
voice unusually high.

I was greatly tempted to throw a jug of water
over her head. But I was even more greatly avid to
see her. I wanted to know about her afternoon with
Edwina. I wanted to know about her affair with
Revisson Doe, and what she would say about her
new job with Sir Quentin. I was also keen to find
out if she had discovered that I had retrieved my
Warrender Chase.

I let her in.

"I came last night," she said. "But you were out."
There was a tone of reproach as she said it, which
made me laugh.

"What is there to laugh about?" said Dottie
as she took off her coat and sat down in my wicker
arm-chair. The manuscript of *Warrender Chase*
was visible on the writing-table and the pages
I had typed were face downwards on the other
side of the typewriter. I had no intention of
hiding the book, but she didn't notice it at the
moment.

"I had a terrible time with that repulsive old
woman," said Dottie.

"Oh, well, you'll have to get used to it," I said.
"Edwina's part of the job, in a sense."

I saw that Dottie was excited and distressed. She
was trembling. I felt rather sorry for her.

"I haven't come to discuss the job," said Dottie. "I
came last night. I came to tell you that Sir Quentin

169

wants those biographies back. I have to work on them. Hand them over, please."

"Have you come here in the middle of the night to fetch them? Don't you see I'm busy?"

"Give me a drink," said Dottie. "I've come for some typing paper. I'm typing Leslie's novel and I've run out of typing paper. I could have sworn I had a new packet of paper, but I can't find it. I must have left it in the shop. I wanted to get on with Leslie's novel because he's coming back from Ireland tomorrow night. He was to be away three weeks, but you know what he is. I won't have time to buy paper tomorrow morning because I'm starting my job tomorrow morning. And Park and Revisson Doe are probably going to publish Leslie's book."

I handed her a whisky and water. I said, "Are you sure you should be drinking? Are you ill?"

She didn't reply. Her eyes were on my *Warrender Chase*.

"What's that?" said Dottie.

"I'm making a few copies of my novel. The old copies got tattered."

"What novel?"

"The same old *Warrender Chase*."

"Where did you get it?" said Dottie.

"Dottie," I said, "you must be mad. What do you mean, where did I get it?"

"How many handwritten copies of the original did you make?" Dottie said.

"Oh, dear," I said. "Don't be boring. Tell me about your affair with Revisson Doe."

170

She spilt her whisky as she put the glass down on the floor.

"You don't understand," she said, "that sometimes a woman has to make a sacrifice for a man. You're hard. You're evil. Why don't you see a priest?"

Now, seeing a priest is all very well if you have something on your conscience. But there are very few predicaments in a writer's life where it would be the slightest use explaining the in's and out's to a priest. A priest is the person to see if you fear for your immortal soul, but not if you are menaced by someone else's. I told Dottie, "I would as soon see a priest about you or, for instance, Sir Quentin, as I would go to consult a doctor about your lungs and his kidneys. Why don't you see a priest, yourself?"

"I will when it's all over," said Dottie. "Leslie needs a publisher."

She was shaking very badly.

I said, "You should see a doctor."

She threw the rest of her whisky all over my typed pages. I got a cloth and blotted them as best I could.

I said, "Sir Quentin Oliver urged you to take on that old man, didn't he?"

"Sir Quentin," she said, "is a genius and a born leader. Now give me those biographies and I'll go."

"You'll go," I said, "but the biographies are staying with me until I've had time to study them. A lot of my *Warrender Chase* has been transferred to those biographies. When I've extracted what's mine I'll hand over the rest."

"What a fiend you are," Dottie said.

I don't know what prompted me then to ask, "Are you taking pills?"

"What pills?" said Dottie.

"Drugs."

"Only for my weight-reducing," said Dottie.

"From a doctor?"

"No, I get them from a friend."

I put together half a ream of typing paper and gave it to Dottie. I told her she was a fool.

She said, "You're furious because I've taken your job."

I said that was fair enough, everything she had done was fair enough, because I had once taken her husband. But she was a fool to have any more to do with the Autobiographical Association.

"Who took me there in the first place?" said Dottie.

"I did, I'm sorry to say. But I tore up your biography as soon as I realized there was something wrong."

Dottie said, "I enjoy sleeping with Revisson Doe."

"Get out, I've got work to do. It's late."

"Have you got a cup of cocoa?"

I made her a cup of cocoa. I gave her the embroidered silk handkerchief-case that I hadn't left at her flat.

"Why don't you give up the idea of being an author?" said the English Rose. "Everything used

172

to be all right between us and Leslie was your friend too. But that mad novel of yours—Sir Quentin says—"

"Out," I breathed, so as not to wake the house. This time she went.

Chapter Eleven

It was not many hours before Dottie discovered that the handwritten copy of my *Warrender Chase* she had seen that night in my room was in fact the one she had stolen; she found the ream of typing paper in her bag under her knitting. She rang me up the next afternoon.

"How did you get into my flat?" she said.

I had already returned the key to Gray Mauser. I didn't anwer her question, I didn't even ask how my novel got into her flat. I hung up.

An hour later she rang again. "Listen, Fleur, Sir Quentin is anxious to have a chat with you."

"Where are you speaking from?"

"I'm at home. I don't think I can manage the job."

"You've fallen out with Sir Quentin."

"Well not exactly, but—"

"He's furious because you didn't destroy my manuscript."

"Well, it deserves to be destroyed."

That evening I finished typing *Warrender Chase*. I had been typing steadily all day; my shoulders ached and I lay on my bed reading it through for typographical errors. I could see its defects as a novel but they weren't the sort of defects that could be removed without removing the entire essence. It's often like that with a novel or a story. One sees a fault or a blemish, perhaps in the portrayal of a character, but cosmetic treatment won't serve; change the setting of a scene and the balance of the whole work is adversely affected. So I left my *Warrender Chase* as it was.

Solly looked in for a drink before he went to his night-work and took away two typed copies of my book, one to send to a publisher and the other to keep in the safe at the office. He said, "You could sue them all, you could give them in charge."

"Would it do my book any good?" I said.

"No," said Solly, "it would only make false publicity. Your novel has to stand on its merits, especially a first novel."

"What should I do with the biographies?"

"Destroy the bits he's lifted from your novel and give him back the rest."

I told Solly that was what I intended to do. But first I was interested to see what use Sir Quentin had put my work to. "I think he's putting my *Warrender Chase* into practice. He's trying to live out my story. I haven't had time to look at the files properly, but that's what I think."

"You can't control his actions," said Solly. "Don't let these people get on your nerves. Just give him back what's his and let him put it away for seventy years. Who cares? You'll get another job, you'll write another book and forget them."

．　．　．

When I lugged out the bag full of the Auto-biographical Association files later that night, and opened it, I began to feel hysterical. The very touch of them seemed to be radio-active with harm. I shuffled through the folders till I came to Lady Bernice "Bucks" Gilbert.

Then the phone rang. What instinct urged me at first not to answer it? It was only eight twenty-five. It rang. It persisted. The house-boy must have known I was in. Possibly he thought I had just gone out to the lavatory and would presently be back in the room. On rang the piercing one-tone signal from the household exchange downstairs. I answered it. I heard the boy say, "Here she is for you." A click, and "Oh Fleur," said Mrs. Tims, "I'm so glad I caught you in. Something has occurred. It's to do with Lady Edwina, she wants to see you."

"Is she ill?"

"I wouldn't say she was well. It's a delicate matter. Can you come at once? Sir Quentin will of course pay for the taxi."

"Put me through to Lady Edwina," I said.

"Oh, I can't do that."

"Why not?"

"She's not in a state."

I asked then to speak to Miss Fisher.

"Nurse Fisher's gone to her sister's."

"Have you called the doctor?"

"Well," said Beryl Tims, "we were debating . . ."

"Don't debate. Send for the doctor," I said.

177

"But she wants you, Fleur."

"Pass me Sir Quentin."

"I doubt he would have anything to say to you, Fleur. Sir Quentin is very offended."

"He owes me my pay and a lot of explanations," I said.

There was a pause while the English Rose evidently covered the receiver to speak to Sir Quentin, for eventually he came on the phone.

"You would do me a great favour," he said, "if you would come and see Mummy. It is quite urgent. Whatever has gone wrong between us, I assue you Miss Talbot, I don't want to come between you and Mummy."

"I want to speak to her."

"Alas, that is not possible."

In the end I went, having first bundled the autobiographies back into my clothes cupboard and locked it. Anyone who has read *Warrender Chase* will know what happened to those autobiographies during my absence. In fact, the possibility was already half in my mind that I was falling into the same trap as Marjorie in my novel when she was called away from Warrender's papers on the pretext that the ancient Prudence needed her. But the very fact that it was half in my mind almost, to the other half of my mind, precluded the possibility that my suspicions could be valid. It seemed quite unlikely that my own novel could be entering into my life to such an extent. I very often err by taking the side of rationality in my distrust of suspicions.

I reached Hallam Street within half an hour.

"Miss Talbot," said Sir Quentin, "would you step into my study for a moment? Mummy has fortunately, most fortunately, dropped off to sleep. It would be such a pity to disturb her after all this, after all this . . ."

"Well that's all right, then," I said. "I don't need to stay."

But he had me by the arm and was propelling me into the study. "Take off your coat, please do, Miss Talbot," said Sir Quentin. "There are just one or two small items we have to discuss."

"If you mean the files of your Association," I said, "I'll discuss them when I've studied them better. So far as I can see you've plagiarized my novel *Warrender Chase.* I assure you that I'll sue."

"Ah, your novel, your novel, I don't know anything about that. I don't wonder you've been unable to give your full attention to your job here with us when you've been scribbling novels at the same time. Delusions of grandeur."

From the other end of the house came a crash and a shriek. "Fleur! Is that you, Fleur? Leave me alone, Tims you bitch. I want to see Fleur. I know she's here. I know that Fleur's in the house."

Sir Quentin continued, "It is I who shall sue."

I sat still, as if agreeing to ignore Edwina's noise.

"The question arises," I said, "why Bernice Gilbert took her life."

"It is I who shall—"

But I had leapt up and got out into the passage

where Edwina was trying to rid herself of Beryl Tims's restraint.

"Fleur, how wonderful to see you, what a surprise," croaked Edwina. "Come along to my room."

I shoved Beryl Tims out of the way and followed Edwina. From the other end of the passage came Sir Quentin's frail cry, "Mummy!"

Before I left Hallam Street that night I got my pay and my employment cards. I also got an envelope from Edwina which she cunningly drew out of her pillow-case and crammed into my coat-pocket, shrieking the while; so that Beryl Tims, who had gone into Edwina's bathroom to get some water for Edwina to take with her sleeping pill, wasn't aware of our transaction.

I promised Edwina I would drop in and see her again very soon. There was always some reason why I couldn't break with Hallam Street once and for all. This put me in mind of those scenes in *Warrender Chase* where my character, the scholar Proudie, repeatedly comes across letters from Marjorie to Warrender making excuses for not being able to come to see him in the country, and yet obviously she has continued to do so right up to the time of Warrender's death in the car crash. When Proudie asks Marjorie why she went back to the house continually, Marjorie says, "I wanted to break. But the Greek girl was helpless there. And Prudence, I had to see Prudence."

I thought of this as I sat in the taxi going home. I

180

remembered the opening scene of my novel, how the group of people are waiting for Warrender to join them. He is late. He doesn't come. He has been killed in a car crash.

My thoughts went like this: Warrender Chase was killed in a car crash while everyone is assembled, waiting for him. Quentin Oliver's destiny, if he wants to enact Warrender Chase, would be the same. It was a frightening thought but at the same time external to me, as if I were watching a play I had no power to stop. It then came to me again, there in the taxi, what a wonderful thing it was to be a woman and an artist in the twentieth century. It was almost as if Sir Quentin was unreal and I had merely invented him, Warrender Chase being a man, a real man on whom I had partly based Sir Quentin. It is true that I felt tight-strung but I remember those sensations very clearly.

That Sir Quentin was real became obvious when I got back to my room. Nothing seemed amiss, it is true. I got the key of the cupboard out of my bag and opened it. Solly's hold-all was in its place. I opened it and gazed into its emptiness, hypnotised by my predicted loss and the extent of my own folly in not having followed my instinct. The mouth of the bag gaped at me, ha-ha. It had been a professional job. There was no sign of a tampering with the lock of my door, no scratches of a bungling amateur on the cupboard. I had to wait till the morning to confirm with the house-boy that nobody to his knowledge had been to see me. No callers in the house at all? He replied with a lot of thunder, from which there flashed like sheet-lightning in my mind the simple fact that I knew already: a professional thief had been employed to come to the house, straight to the spot where I kept the biographies. The lay-out was known to Dottie, and plainly it was she who, unwittingly perhaps, had provided the neat information. That night, I looked for my *Warrender Chase* in a suitcase under the bed where I now kept it. In my anxious state I had forgotten that I had abstracted the original manuscript before I had gone out; I had put this under my pillow. So that in the suitcase I found only the spare copy of the new transcript, the two others of which I had given to Solly. But where, where, were my foolscap manuscript pages? I searched my room for an hour and it wasn't till I got into bed that I felt them under my pillow.

This brought to mind the envelope Edwina had thrust into my coat-pocket. I jumped out of bed, quite refreshed and strengthened by this exciting recollection; I'm one of those people who can quickly recover from physical exhaustion if they are in the least stimulated mentally. The blank and crumpled envelope contained some handwritten pages evidently torn out of a diary. They had been torn roughly, so that some of the words at the beginning of each line were partly missing and equally at the end of the lines on the reverse sides. It seemed to me that the handwriting was Sir Quentin's and as I read the first page it was plain that the diary entries were his.

26th April, 1950.

I have gained the confidence
Miss Talbot's friend, Dorothy
ottie", Mrs. Carpenter, with
whose husband, Leslie, Miss Talbot
ad an affair.
"Dottie" has obtained for
the printed proofs of a novel
titled "Warrender Chase" as an
xample of a morbid literary production which in her ("Dottie"'s)
pinion should be suppressed.
I have read this production
Miss Talbot's inflamed and in-
ne imagination. That such an one
hould have entered my ken!!
The book is an attempted *roman
à clef* if ever there was one!
Query: Is Miss T. a mind-reader?
a medium?
? Evil

I turned over the page:

28th April, 1950.

"Dottie" informed me that tw
Authors, Theodore Clairmont an
his wife Audrey (N.B. not list

in "Who's Who") have read the
so-called novel. They vehementl
disapprove of that same. I was
informed that the piece of wri
already in printers' proof, is
be published by Messrs. Park,
Revisson Doe, a minor but recogni
establishment.

I have consequently made a
rendez-vous with a director of
firm, Mr. Revisson Doe himself.
(N.B. Nothing in "Burke's", "Haydn,
etc. etc. Undistinguished entry in
"Who's Who".)

Next page:

1st May, 1950.

As a result of my visit to the
emises of Park, Revisson Doe,
is afternoon, when I saw Mr.
evisson Doe himself in his office
stressed the seriousness of the
bellous aspect of the novel so-
alled by Miss Fleur Talbot *vis
vis* my Autobiographical Asscn.

He promptly agreed to withdraw
the novel from publication. (The
hreat of libel is never-failing
ith these people.) I judged Mr.
e to be a sound business man but

f no family antecedents to speak
f.

He mentioned that "Dottie" had
shown him some chapters of a novel
 hich her husband is writing, quite
a *tour de force* in which his past
 elations with a young ambitious
 emale were, to those "in the know"
 idently an account of his doings
 ith the redoubtable Fleur Talbot!!

1st May [contd]

He remarked that "Dottie"
was "a very pretty girl." He
remarked that he used this phrase
"as man to man," which I appreci-
ated. I commented that I would do
my best to further his interest i
"Dottie" at which we enjoyed som
innocent laughter. I expressed m
gratitude for his co-operation and
assured him of mine.

Before I left Mr. Doe offered
to "confirm in writing" his undertaking to scrap the contract for
the said "Warrender Chase". I beg
him not to make any written record
of our *tête à tête,* assuring him tha
on my part any written record would
be merely a note assigned to a loc
drawer for seventy years. I proffered
this information true to my princi
of complete frankness.

2nd May, 1950.

Pleasurable sensations: Early this
orning, walking in the Park I observ-
d a striped cat among the shrubbery,
orming as it were a pattern with the
pale light and the shadows of the wet
eaves. How nature is at one! I was
ellbound, rapt within a magic ring,
assive, receptive, all knowing.
I thought in that moment 'twere sweet
to die. My dearest, I would that we
could die together. Had I not my
Mission which I, and I alone, am subtly
illed to fulfil. But who are your
riends? Where are they?
Be not discomfited. I etc. etc.

Above letter to Bucks?

Yes, I have done it. And delivered
it!! But

Now what infuriated me more than anything in
these scraps of Quentin Oliver's diary was this last
entry, 2nd May. It was straight out of *Warrender
Chase*, where I make my character Proudie find the
absurd letter to the Greek girl who thought it far
from absurd.

When I had got over my fury at this raid on my
Warrender Chase I put the diary papers back into
their envelope and stuffed it down at the bottom of

186

my hand-bag, determined never to part with it. To whatever use I might put the knowledge it conveyed, I felt relieved to know with precision what I had obscurely suspected. Also, I was highly amused at the thought of Sir Quentin's discovery of the missing leaves of his diary. I was sure he would imagine I had hired a professional burglar. This amused me greatly and I fell asleep rejoicing.

Next morning I had an interview for a job at the B.B.C., which I didn't get. I sat at a long board-room table with many men and women to ask me questions. But I didn't have the required experience and, said the most elderly of the men, did I realize that the six pounds a week that I was asking was three hundred pounds a year? I said I thought it was three hundred and twelve. Anyway, I didn't get the job. I certainly wasn't looking my best. A little later on in my life when my fortunes had changed and I was writing for the B.B.C., my new friends on the production side fell upon the official file in which that interview was duly recorded and we all made merry of it.

I typed out a fair copy of those leaves of Sir Quentin's diary and took them along at tea-time to Hallam Street.

Undoubtedly he was a lunatic. I felt sure that was what Edwina had intended to convey by giving me those torn-out sheets.

"Lady Edwina is asleep," said Beryl Tims. "But

you needn't bother to come and see her any more. There's nothing in it for you. We've made a discovery, and do you know what that is?—We've discovered that she has no money at all, not to leave to anybody. She bought an annuity and when she dies the money dies with her. She's very, very, cunning, that's the word. Sir Quentin has only just found out. Her fortune's all a myth."

I had known this for a long time, for one Sunday when I was wheeling Edwina out with Solly she told me, "I married for money."

"I consider that very immoral of you, Edwina," said Solly.

"I don't see why. My husband married me for money. We were a devoted couple. We had several things in common. One was expensive tastes and the other was no money."

She had then rambled on about Quentin "coming as a surprise" and "his own father, of course" had provided for him and a little for Edwina. So that we were fairly in the air as to Quentin's parentage, and we left Edwina's story at that, all charming as it was and unspoiled by explanations.

"Not a penny," the English Rose was saying, "beyond her annuity, which just covers her own keep and the nurse."

Miss Fisher came out of the kitchen just then. "Good-afternoon, Fleur. Lady Edwina will be delighted to see you. She's getting up for tea."

I said I'd come in as soon as I'd seen Sir Quentin. Mrs. Tims said, "You want Sir Quentin? Well—"

188

I opened the study door and found him at his desk, staring into space.

"Is your new secretary here?" I said.

"Why, Miss Talbot. I— She had to go home early." He waved me to a chair.

"Read this," I said, putting the typed pages of his diary in front of him. I continued standing.

He looked at the first page and said, "Where did you get this?"

"From your diary. I have the pages."

"How did you get at my diary?"

"I have professional help. The originals are locked in a bank vault. Maybe for seventy years, maybe not."

He got up and started walking round the room, putting things straight. He stopped and looked at the other pages I had typed. He gave a laugh. "Why, that diary is a little joke of mine. There's nothing serious in it."

I said, "You will have to see a psychiatrist. That's number one. Second, you must wind up the Autobiographical Association. If you don't do both by the end of the month I shall make a fuss."

"Ah, but the members themselves will have something to say about that."

I left him and went to see Edwina where she was propped up for tea in the drawing-room, wrapped in an Indian shawl. Sir Quentin came in with a leather-bound book in his hand, his diary. He was followed by Beryl Tims.

"Mummy," he said, "I want you to know that

your friend Miss Fleur Talbot is not our friend. She belongs to the underworld. She has arranged for a professional thief to enter this house and abstract some pages from my private diary. On her own admission. Miss Fisher, have you missed anything? Is Lady Edwina's jewellery intact?"

Edwina stood up and wet the floor.

"Miss Talbot, I must ask you to leave this house."

"No harm in asking," said Edwina. "I pay the rent. Your home is in the country, Quentin."

Miss Fisher came mopping up round Edwina who finally agreed to be taken back to her room to be tidied up. I waited for her return, helping myself to a sandwich, while Sir Quentin simply stared at me and Beryl Tims moved the plate of sandwiches out of my reach.

The door-bell rang and Beryl Tims went to answer it. "You are a fiend," said Sir Quentin. "Your enthusiasm for John Henry Cardinal Newman was pure hypocrisy. Did he not form under his influence a circle of devoted spiritual followers? Am I not entitled to do the same?"

"But you know," I said, "you're off your head. You had this desire to take possession of people before I came along and reminded you of the existence of Newman. You've read my novel, but only recently. You must see a psychiatrist and break up the Association."

I could hear voices in the hall. I went out to say good-bye to Edwina and on the way I saw that the two new visitors were the Baronne Clotilde and Father Delaney, both looking extremely haggard yet not pitiable. These two were always arrogant, insolent in their folly.

In Edwina's room, where the nurse was rummaging in her wardrobe for another wonderful dress, I said, "I've told him to see a mental doctor and disband his troupe."

"Quite right," said Edwina. "When am I going to meet your friend Wally?"

"I'll arrange it soon."

"Wally and Solly," she cackled with delight. "Don't you think that's a nice couple of names, Nurse?"

"Very nice. Like on the stage." Then Miss Fisher said to me, "I'm concerned about the Dexedrine."

I didn't locate the word Dexedrine precisely. I thought she meant some medicine for Edwina. I said, "Would you like me to take a prescription—?"

"Oh, no. It's the Dexedrine that Sir Quentin gives to his friends. Didn't he give you some?"

"Not me."

"He does the others. It can be dangerous if the dose is high."

"They are all of age. I can't feel sorry for them. They can surely look after themselves."

"Well yes, and no," said the good nurse.

Edwina was impatient to get into her purple dress. "They're all on a fast. Except himself and Tims. And we like our food too, don't we, Nurse?"

"Dexedrine," the nurse explained, "is an appetite suppressor. But it affects the brain."

"Watching their figures," yelled Edwina. "They'll go off their heads."

"Presumably they all have friends," I said. "I suppose they have friends and relations who will notice if they fall ill."

"It still fits," said Edwina, patting her dress.

"There's nothing you can prove," said Miss Fisher, "but I know. Those poor people—"

"They are not infants," I said.

I was thinking of my novel, *Warrender Chase*; now I had no publisher, thanks to Quentin Oliver. I was impatient with his bunch of self-indulgent fools—I thought of Maisie Young with so many possibilities in her life, ready to sacrifice them all in the name of a mad spiritual leader; and the Baronne Clotilde du Loiret, so stunned by privilege that she didn't know how to discern and reject a maniac.

I went home to get ready for a dinner date with Wally. But I didn't say a word to him about Hallam Street. Instead I told him about the B.B.C.; and arising from this—I forget by what route—he told me about getting demobilized from the army, how he and his friends all went along to an army centre which was a group of huts, and there they chose their de-mob clothes. Wally described in detail the range and styles of de-mob suits. He himself had taken a tweed coat and flannel trousers. "Perfectly all right," said Wally in his casual and comfortable way.

It was good to be reminded that there were other things in life besides *Warrender Chase* and the Autobiographical Association. But part of my mind was really elsewhere. I was longing to get home and read Newman. I wanted to see what these people could possibly be making of him. I was interested in that.

But Wally came home with me for a good-night drink. He loved my book-laden room.

"There's a drunk in the street singing 'Auld Lang Syne,'" said Wally. "She seems to be happy, doesn't she?"

I let her sing on.

In the morning before I was up, Dottie was at my door. She had the nerve to bring her black bag with her knitting, now a dark green sweater.

"I came round last night. Your light was on."

"I know."

"Was Leslie here?"

"Go to hell."

"Listen," said Dottie, "I've got to tell you. Sir Quentin has ordered us all to go to his house in Northumberland. He says we're being persecuted here in London, and he's going to make his house into a sort of monastery."

"Like Newman at Littlemore?"

"Exactly. You must admit there's something in Sir Quentin's aims."

I couldn't see any resemblance between Newman and his band of Oxford Anglo-Catholics in their austere retreat at Littlemore, and Sir Quentin with his bunch of cranks. It is true that Newman suffered some real religious and political persecution for his views, and that he also suffered from a sense of persecution not always coinciding with a cause. Nothing else of Newman's matched the Hallam Street set.

I said to Dottie, "One would think that Quentin Oliver had heard of only two books. One is Newman's *Apologia* and the other is my *Warrender Chase*. He's obsessed."

"He believes you're a witch, an evil spirit whose been sent to bring ideas into his life. It's his mission to turn evil to good. I think there's a lot in what he says," Dottie said.

"Well you can put the kettle on," I said, "for I haven't had my breakfast."

She filled the kettle and put it on the gas ring.

"They're going to Northumberland, all except me."

"You have to stay and keep Revisson Doe happy, of course," I said.

"Was Leslie here last night?"

"My business," I said.

"My husband," said Dottie. "He's mine."

"Why don't you rent him out by the hour?"

"I wish I could go to Northumberland," Dottie said. "Sir Quentin phoned urgently to everyone. They're all going. Maisie rang me. She's going. Father Delaney—"

"It's the best news I've heard for a long time," I said. "What about Edwina?"

"Oh they're not taking her. She'll stay in London with the nurse. You might as well know, if you don't know already, that she won't have anything to leave when she dies."

I said, and I don't know why I said it (but I was thinking of my character, old Prudence, who inherited my Warrender's estate), "she might outlive her son and inherit the lot."

"You and your *Warrender Chase*," observed Dottie, making the tea.

"Are you taking Dexedrine?" I said.

"No, I've stopped. My doctor made me stop. That's why I can't go to Northumberland, in fact. Sir Quentin wouldn't have me."

"Is Beryl Tims going with them?"

"Of course. She acts as High Priestess at the rites. They're leaving right away. I don't know what to do."

"Forget them," I said.

"It's easy for you to forget."

"No it isn't. One day I'll write about all this."

I thought of Cellini: "All men, whatever be their condition . . . should write the tale of their life with their own hand."

"You've already written it," Dottie said, clanking down her tea-cup. "You know your *Warrender Chase* is all about us. You foresaw it all."

"Don't be ridiculous."

When she had packed up her knitting and gone I turned up the passage I wanted in Newman's lovely *Apologia*.

> . . . I recognised what I had to do, though I shrank from both the task and the exposure which it would entail. I must, I said, give the true key to my whole life; I must show what I

195

am that it may be seen what I am not, and that the phantom may be extinguished which gibbers instead of me. I wish to be known as a living man, and not as a scarecrow which is dressed up in my clothes. . . .

And I set it on the table against my Benvenuto Cellini:

All men, whatever be their condition, who have done anything of merit, or which verily has a semblance of merit, if so be they are men of truth and good repute, should write the tale of their life with their own hand.

I looked from one to another, admiring both. I thought that, one day, when the months between the autumn of 1949 and the summer of 1950 should become long ago and I should have achieved something which "verily has a semblance of merit," I would set it forth. I was in a state of acute happiness at Dottie's news. I needed a job and my novel needed a publisher. But in the departure of the Autobiographical Association I felt I had escaped from it. Although in reality I wasn't yet rid of Sir Quentin and his little sect, they were morally outside of myself, they were objectified. I would write about them one day. In fact, under one form or another, whether I have liked it or not, I have written about them ever since, the straws from which I have made my bricks.

Chapter Twelve

It was right in the middle of the twentieth century, the last day of June 1950, warm and sunny, a Friday, that I mark as a changing-point in my life. That goes back to the day I took my sandwiches to the old disused Kensington graveyard to write a poem with my lunch, when the young policeman sauntered over to see what I was up to. He was a clean-cut man, as on war memorials. I asked him: suppose I had been committing a crime sitting there on the gravestone, what crime would it be? "Well, it could be desecrating and violating," he said, "it could be obstructing and hindering without due regard, it could be loitering with intent." I offered him a sandwich but he refused; he had just had his dinner himself. "The graves must be very old," said the policeman. He wished me the best of luck and went on his way. I forget what poem I was writing at the time, but it was probably an exercise in a fixed form, such as a rondeau, triolet or villanelle; also, I was practising Alexandrines for narrative verse about that time, so it might have been one of those; I always found the practise of metre and form for their own sake very absorbing and often, all at once, inspiring. I was waiting till my landlord, Mr. Alexander, should be out of the way with his fussing over my overcrowded room.

I couldn't afford to take a larger room, I could hardly afford to pay the rent for my small room. I had found some work, reading manuscripts and proof-reading for the publisher in Wapping, I did some reviewing of poetry and stories. I was also well ahead with my second novel, *All Souls' Day,* and had already planned my third, *The English Rose. Warrender Chase* was still unpublished in spite of Solly's efforts and in fact I had given up hope of its being published; all my hopes were on *All Souls' Day.* But my savings were running low and I knew I would have to start selling my books. I was seriously looking for a full-time job.

But that day in the middle of the twentieth century I felt more than ever how good it was to be a woman and an artist there and then. I had been depressed most of the past six weeks, but now it all suddenly passed, as depressions do.

My week-end at Wally's cottage at Marlow on the day after petrol-rationing was lifted, the twenty-seventh of May, had been, not quite a disaster, but certainly a mess.

It had started off very well, when I took Wally to Hallam Street to breakfast with Edwina before we set off. Sir Quentin had already fled to Northumberland and Edwina was alone with Miss Fisher and a new daily help. Edwina had decked herself out in egg-shell blue trimmed with swansdown that moulted considerably over our breakfast; the colour-scheme was repeated on her eyelids. She must have started preparations for the breakfast some hours before. Her hands were heavily laden with rings and tipped with the brightest varnish.

"Are you Fleur's boy-friend?" she yelled at Wally.

"Yes."

"She's too good for you."

"Yes, I know," said Wally in that genial way of his.

We sat at a small lacy table set in the window of her own small sitting-room. She was alert, happy to have her flat to herself, and she enchanted Wally by her anecdotes about the late Arthur Balfour. When I asked her if Beryl Tims intended to remain in Northumberland, she said, "Beryl who?" I didn't see Edwina again until the following week when I wheeled her, all in heavy black with her string of pearls, into her son Quentin's funeral service.

Wally was greatly taken with Edwina, as he told me on the way to Marlow. "I'm in love with your Edwina," he said. At Marlow Wally was upset to find that the woman who came to clean up had not been near the place. I think what annoyed him most was my seeing the evidence of a previous week-end for two. I really didn't mind because the situation itself was a lively one; I do dearly love a turn of events. But I couldn't help wondering who the other girl had been and, observing the mouse-nibbled, greenish crusts of the last breakfast toast on the floor, the black-rimmed green milk in the jug, the two coffee cups and saucers on the draining board, caked with hardened coffee, dry and old, I calculated the age of this evidence; how many week-ends ago, and what had I been doing with Wally the weekdays in between? As Wally stood and swore, I dumped my week-end case in the bedroom with a myopic airiness. The bed was very much crumpled for two, and as if by a competent stage-manager, Wally's blue cotton py-jama top hung on the bed-post while the trousers lay, neat and unfolded, on the top of the chest of drawers. A near-empty bottle of whisky and two glasses, one lipstick-stained, were decidedly over-done from the point of view of scenic production, but they were there. We cleared up the place and went out for lunch.

Towards evening I was taken with an attack of nervousness, for no apparent reason, about my almost-forgotten *Warrender Chase*. I was wondering if I had handled that opening scene as well as I might. I had typed and retyped the novel so many times I almost knew it by heart.

"You know, Fleur," said Wally. "Sometimes when I'm with you, a very odd thing happens— you're suddenly *not there*. It's creepy. Very often, even when I don't say anything, I feel somehow, you're somewhere else."

I laughed, because I knew he was right. I said, "I've been thinking about my first novel, *Warrender Chase*, it's preying on my mind."

200

"Oh, don't let it do that. I've had ideas for novels myself, but I really haven't the time."

"Do you think you could write a novel?"

"Oh, if one had the time I daresay one could write as good a novel as the next chap."

He went out to call at his cleaning woman's house to find out what was the matter with her. He had got over his earlier embarrassment but the week-end already seemed to me to have gone flat. Perhaps we had both been looking forward to it too much. It is as true as any of the copy-book maxims, that love is by nature unforeseen. And I was now so far away in my thoughts that I could only note in his absence that I had a soft spot for Wally, anyway.

We had brought some food with us. I began to set the table for supper and I lit two candles, but I was so abstracted that I can't remember now anything but a general impression of his cottage, or anything about what we had to eat. I think there was a gramophone and that I put on a record.

My mind was unaccountably on *Warrender Chase*, the opening scene where Warrender's mother Prudence, his nephew Roland and Charlotte the frightful housekeeper are waiting for Warrender's arrival in the drawing-room of Warrender's house in the country.

Roland has been playing with one of the South American Indian masks that Warrender collects. Charlotte takes it away from him: "Your uncle doesn't like it if anyone touches his odds and ends." Marjorie, Roland's wife, has just answered the

201

telephone in the hall, dashed out and driven off. Prudence keeps saying, "Where did Marjorie go?" and "Roland, go and see what's happened to Marjorie. Take the bicycle." Roland is talking about the adding machines he's selling on a commission basis. Charlotte says she isn't interested in adders. Then she says, all right, adding machines. She says, things are getting to a point where they have nothing to add because Warrender is short of money with too many people to support. Prudence points out that the machines also subtract. She says Warrender has been pronouncing words in a new way. They all discuss the new way. "Dense" instead of "dance," inter*est*ing, "lawst" for "lost." Charlotte comes in with the observation that "Mr. Proudie speaks like that." "Proudie's diction is not all that's to be desired of a scholar," says Prudence. "However, we may assume that Warrender has been seeing a lot of Proudie. I'm anxious about Marjorie, running off wildly after that telephone call. And Warrender should be here by now. Where has he got to?"

Then I made my character Charlotte go to the window. "I can hear his car coming." Roland says, "No, I'm sure it's Marjorie's car. Warrender's car goes *tum*-te-te-tum. Marjorie's goes tum, tum, *tum*-te-te like this one."

Prudence says, "Roland, stop playing with that mask, just to oblige me. Warrender paid a lot for it. I know it's a fake, but so is Warrender." Marjorie comes into the room. "What's the matter, Marjorie?" "Oh, she's ill, give her a drink, water,

202

something." "Marjorie, what happened? That phone call. Are you hurt?" At last Marjorie says, "Warrender is hurt. The car crashed. He's terribly hurt. The police rang here. I went to the hospital. I couldn't identify him at first. His face, Warrender's face . . ." She passes her hand over her own face and says, "I think his face is quite demolished." Roland here goes out to telephone the hospital. Charlotte: "Is he dead?" Marjorie: "No, he's still unconscious, I'm afraid." Now Charlotte, the English Rose, seizes on those words "unconscious, I'm afraid." "What do you mean, you're afraid? Do you want him to die?"

Roland comes back: "He's dead."

Wally's car pulled up and he came in smiling. "Mrs. Richards had an op. Good thing I called round. She can't work for a few weeks yet. She's awfully reliable, I knew something had happened. Nothing serious, anyway, she didn't show me the op. The men always do."

I said, "Did I tell you the Autobiographical Association has moved to Northumberland to Sir Quentin's house?"

"Oh forget them, Fleur. It was a lousy job. Not your thing at all from the sound of it. Edwina's well out of it too. Awful for her, having a crack-pot for a son. Maybe she's too old to care."

Now I decided to force *Warrender Chase* out of my mind. To do so I began to tell Wally about my new novel, *All Souls' Day*. I think he was fairly interested. After supper we went down to the pub for a drink. We walked home by the river and so to

203

bed. It was simply no good. Anxious not to be abstracted and "not there" with Wally, my mind was now only too deliberately concentrated on the actuality of the occasion. I found myself vigilant of every detail in Wally's love-making, I was noticing, I was *counting*. I was single-mindedly conscious. In desperation I tried thinking of General de Gaulle, which made matters worse, far, far, worse.

"I'm afraid I've had too much beer," said poor Wally.

Next morning we went out on the river for an hour. After lunch we tidied up the cottage and set off early for London. Wally dropped me at my house just after five in the afternoon.

Dottie again, at midnight. I put on my dressing gown and let her in. "Sir Quentin's been killed in a car accident. A head-on collision last night," she said.

"What about the other car? Anyone hurt?"

"Oh, they were killed too," said Dottie with the impatience that denoted she was dealing with an imbecile who couldn't distinguish the kernel from the nutshell.

"How many in the other car?"

"Two, I think, but the point is—"

"Thank God he's dead," I said.

"So that it proves your *Warrender Chase* to be valid."

"Nothing to do with my *Warrender Chase*. Quite a different situation. The man was pure evil."

"They were all waiting for him to join them," Dottie said. I got rid of Dottie.

The theme of *Warrender Chase* was indeed valid. Such events as I'd portrayed, even in a different way from the reality, could happen. My *Warrender Chase* was valid, and I decided that my Chapter One, which had haunted me at Wally's cottage, could very well stand as it was.

At ten the next morning I rang Miss Fisher at Hallam Street. Edwina, she said, had taken the news very bravely. The doctor had been to see her. Everything was all right, and Edwina was keeping very quiet.

After the funeral Beryl Tims caught up with me and said, in Edwina's hearing, "You'll have to work out something with Lady Edwina. Sir Quentin's property reverts to her and I have no settlement."

"Edwina," I said, "Mrs. Tims is here to present her condolences."

"I noticed her," said Edwina.

I wheeled her away, upright as she was, in her glittering black. What shocked me was that Beryl Tims had used almost the very words of my Charlotte, at Warrender's funeral.

From the day of the funeral to the day at the end of June when I sat in the graveyard writing my poem, Dottie kept me abundantly informed about the members of the disbanded Association.

"We were wondering," Dottie said, "what had happened to the biographies. They never got a chance to read them."

"Edwina destroyed them."

"Had she a right to do that?"

"I suppose so."

"She wasn't by any chance influenced by you?"

"No, she just told me she'd got Miss Fisher to destroy the papers. Nothing of any interest, and she hadn't the space to hoard them."

"Poor Beryl Tims. He promised to make a settlement on her. Do you know that Eric Findlay has gone back to his wife?"

"I didn't know he'd left her."

"Well, Fleur, he left her for you. It was in his autobiography. You had an affair with him, Fleur. I saw it written down in black and white. Sir Quentin showed it to me."

"Was it written in his own hand?"

"No, well of course, Sir Quentin took it down verbally. He wrote it for Eric."

"Well, it wasn't true. He invented it."

"It's just possible," said Dottie, "that it wasn't true. On the other hand—"

"Get out."

So it went on. Maisie Young had a nervous break-down and got over it, all in those few weeks between the funeral and my special day in the graveyard. Clotilde du Loiret had gone to stay at a convent in France to find her soul, which she felt she had lost. Dottie was seeing a lot of Father Delaney who enjoyed taking her to wrestling matches and who was still consuming Dexedrine. Mrs. Wilks had gone back to her family, but visited Sir Quentin's grave every day, where she conversed with him. When I asked Dottie if anyone visited Bucks Gilbert's grave, she said, "Oh, well, suicide's a mortal sin. She shouldn't have had a Christian burial."

I saw Edwina frequently all that month of June. And Wally, too; he wanted to take me back to Marlow for a better week-end. But I had to work all my week-ends at my reviewing and my new novel, knowing that soon I would have to take a full-time job.

The day after I met the policeman at the Kensington graveyard was Saturday the first of July. Now began my new life. I got a letter from the great and glorious Triad Press, an old establishment which specialized in publishing books of good quality. It was a simple letter:

> Dear Miss Talbot,
>   We would be grateful if you would make an appointment to visit us here, at your earliest convenience.
>
> Yours sincerely,
>
> Cynthia Somerville
> The Triad Press.

Now, Edwina had rambled about the Somervilles of Triad, whose great-uncle she had known. She had thought I might get a job there. Solly, it now came to mind, had also said to me, "You might get a job at Triad." It occurred to me that either Edwina or Solly had recommended me for a job. I checked with both of them the next afternoon. We didn't take Edwina out for a walk that Sunday. I think it rained. We had tea at Hallam Street. Edwina had now added to her staff a handsome, sturdy manservant, a widower called Rudder, who had been a butler in a grand house before the war and a sergeant-major in the army. He managed the rations so well that Edwina was able to offer us teas on a grand scale.

"No, I haven't said anything to Triad," said Solly, turning over the letter as if it held some secret code. Nor did Edwina seem to know anything about it.

"Maybe it's about that book of yours, Miss Fleur," said Rudder, who was quite one of the family. Indeed, according to Dottie, he was getting "very thick" with Miss Fisher and both of them were quite milking Edwina; that was according to Dottie, but I didn't see that it mattered since Edwina was so well suited by them both. Rudder now had the letter in his hand. "It looks to me like they want your book. You see they say grateful. Now, if you go after a position it's never the employer that's grateful, it's you that's grateful. You see, here, they've written 'We would be grateful if you would make—'"

"My God," said Solly, "I sent them *Warrender Chase* four, five weeks ago. I forgot."

"I hope they're grateful enough," Edwina croaked.

For the rest of the tea Solly described the Triad trio. Two brothers and a sister. They did everything in unison.

208

"But you'd better not build up your hopes," Solly said. "It could be only about a job. They might have heard from someone you're looking for a job and there might just be a vacancy."

"Well, even that would be something," I said.

It wasn't about a job. It was about *Warrender Chase*.

The famous trio were sitting side by side at a desk. They were Leopold, Cynthia and Claude Somerville themselves, arbiters of taste and of *belles-lettres*. I think they shared a soul. Their mournful grey-green eyes were identical, their long oval faces very similar. Leopold, the youngest, in his early thirties, gave a little jump in his chair when he had something to say which excited him. Cynthia sat perfectly still with her hands clasped before her. She wore a grey-green dress which picked up the colour of the six Somerville eyes; her sleeves were wide, with a mediaeval look. Claude was the eldest, with greying hair; it fell to Claude to discuss the business side which he did with such an air of apologetic and timid regret as to make it positively cruel to question or discuss the terms of the contract which I rejoiced to notice he had ready on the desk before him.

Their long desk as sheer and shiny, no blotting pads, no pen-stands, no In and Out trays. Only my *Warrender Chase* lying in front of Cynthia, a fil which contained readers' reports in front of Leopold and the contract in front of Claude. The were ready for their portrait to be painted. Th had everything except a *Brandenburg Concerto* in the background. But I'm sure they didn't arrange themselves as consciously as appeared. There was indeed a certain amount of stage-production about the Triad, but as I came to learn throughout the years, their joint and public face was sheer instinct, even genius.

They rose to greet me and sat down again, Leopold with an extra little jump.

"We would be happy to publish your novel," said Cynthia. The siblings smiled in unison, not a wide smile but a kindly one.

It would have been difficult for me to realize at that moment that Cynthia was in fact having an affair with a fruit-loader at Covent Garden, Leopold was chasing a band-leader and Claude was already married to a rich American widow with four children of her own and two of his. To me it seemed the Triad had come into being out of nothing and, when I should depart, to nothing they would return.

Leopold, patting the file of readers' reports, assured me that these were so mixed as to be stimulating from a publisher's point of view. He jumped in his chair and said, "Some readers hated it but some readers loved it." "So we think it will have a small cult-following," said Cynthia. "It will not be a commercial venture, of course," added Claude. "The general consensus," said Leopold, "is that although the evil of Warrender is a shade over-accentuated, you have a universal theme." (Jump.)

I said I thought it possible that there were people like Warrender Chase in real life.

The three assented to this in unison. I felt sure that among the readers who had hated the book were Theo and Audrey Clairmont who sometimes read for the Triad Press; and years later I found that the very excess of their attempts to suppress *Warrender Chase* had finally persuaded the Triad in its favour.

I wanted to take the contract away to study it, a reasonable desire. But it would have been beyond me, beyond anyone I knew, to stab gentle, tentative Claude with so profound a knife-wound. I signed it on the spot, only checking first to see if there was an option clause. Claude noticed my glance. "The option is on terms to be agreed," he murmured, as if with breathless hope that I wouldn't change my mind. And he added, "We consider that wording to be the most tactful." He stressed the word tactful, with the result that tact was temporarily cancelled from the contract-signing scene.

But in fact, it was a good contract. The advance on royalties was an unheard-of hundred pounds, which I needed. I addressed Cynthia as I told them about my forthcoming *All Souls' Day* and the novel I had planned to follow it, *The English Rose.* She looked at me with her grey-green eyes, Claude sighed with wonder and Leopold jumped twice. So began my long career as a novelist with the Triad Press.

I spun out the money till November when

Warrender Chase was to be published. A bad month for publishing, but first novels of uncertain futures had to give precedence to certainties. I corrected the proofs of the book, feeling altogether bored with it. I had nearly finished my *All Souls' Day* which I loved with all my heart in those months.

I think it was in September that Wally took me on a visit to Cambridge. We went to Grantchester, the home of Rupert Brooke. "Stands the church clock at ten to three?" The church clock *stood* at ten to three. By order of the management. I had a sudden revulsion against the clock, Grantchester, Rupert Brooke and the ethos of honey still for tea, and I said so at length to Wally. He was not altogether insensitive. He said, "I hope you don't include me in the whole shooting-match."

Wally eventually married an English Rose who knew all about *placement* and protocol and was admired by everybody including the children's nanny. In time Wally became an ambassador with a swimming pool which was always surrounded by notable people and their consorts to whom Wally would descend from time to time: "I've just got away."

The Triad Press had printed a thousand copies of *Warrender Chase*, reckoning to sell five hundred. "But we can count on some nice reviews," said Cynthia on the telephone. They sent a photographer to my room to take my picture for the back of the jacket cover.

In late October Leslie's novel, *Two Ways,*

appeared. It had a portrait of a hard-hearted woman conflicting with a poor Cockney boy for the affections of our hero. My main objection to it was the diction. Leslie was so hard pressed for ways in which to express an idiom that he had fallen back on phonetic spelling, always a literary defect in my opinion. "'Ow can yer do this ter me guv'ner?" pleads Leslie's young Cockney. When all he had to say (since the reader already knows he's a Cockney) is, "You can't do this." Which is far more authentic to the ear than all the "'ows," "yers" and "ters."

Anyway, Leslie's book got two reviews which Dottie brought round to display to me. They were rather feeble, but better than nothing.

Nothing is what happened to *Warrender Chase* for the first two weeks after it was published. I was saddened by this silence, but not very deeply, for I had half forgotten the book, so much more did I prize my new work.

I went over to Solly one Thursday afternoon. He had promised to lend me some money to pay my rent, for I was waiting to be paid for some reviews and articles. In fact I also owed money to a dentist whose receptionist was beginning to lose patience; I had refused to answer the telephone all day, convinced as I was that the persistent calls were from her. The house-boy was quite offended when I told him on the switchboard to say I was out to everybody. He said he didn't like telling lies. I told him that Not at Home wasn't a lie. He agreed, technically, but he sounded sulky.

213

Solly was sitting among his usual mess of news-papers and journals. I said, "I don't like having to borrow. But I'll pay you back soon."

"You should worry," said Solly. He was smiling in the midst of the papers spread out on his desk and on the chair. There were several weeklies. I saw the *Evening Standard,* too, and then I saw my photograph. Reviews of *Warrender Chase* had ap-peared all over the place, all quite favourable, all very large. Solly said he had advance information from the Sunday papers that the same thing was going to happen there. The *Evening Standard* picture had the caption, "Fleur Talbot in the book-lined study of her town-house." It was all a long time ago.

I recall that Theo Clairmont was one of the Sunday reviewers. He said it was undoubtedly an important book, but the author would probably never be able to write another. The prophecy didn't come to pass, for *All Souls' Day* gave as much pleasure as *Warrender Chase,* and after that, *The English Rose* and the others, some more, some less.

Another thing I recall, that day when I went over to Solly to borrow the money for my rent: on my return there was Mr. Alexander at the door to greet me with a great welcome and a copy of the *Evening Standard* in his hand. He asked me in to have a drink with his wife. I said, another time. The house-boy was also very agitated, not knowing what to do with the phone messages and yet mesmerized by my picture in the paper. He was

214

not quite convinced that I wasn't involved in some wrong-doing.

And I remember Leslie paid me a visit that evening. He congratulated me on my piece of luck. He said, "Of course, a popular success . . ." and didn't finish the sentence. He said, "Well, I'll always be your friend," as if I were out on bail.

The telephone messages had been mounting up. I had a bunch of them from the house-boy, and yet another bunch by nine o'clock that night. I took them to bed with me, feeling somewhat bewildered. I looked them over one by one. Some of the people I was to ring back were Miss Maisie Young, Mrs. Beryl Tims, Miss Cynthia Somerville of the Triad Press, Mr. Gray Mauser, the features editor of *Good Housekeeping*, the literary editor of the *Evening News*, Mr. Tim Sutcliffe of the Third Programme, B.B.C., Mr. Revisson Doe; and there were many others including Dottie.

I rang Dottie back. She accused me of having plotted and planned it all. "You knew what you were doing," she said. I agreed I had been loitering with intent and said I was leaving for Paris in the morning.

In fact, I took refuge with Edwina in Hallam Street for a few weeks till the fuss died down. I had work to do. Success is a subject like any other subject, and I knew too little about it, just then, to be able to discuss it and answer questions about it. In those weeks the Triad sold the American rights, the paperback rights, the film rights, and most of the foreign rights of *Warrender Chase*. Good-bye, my poverty. Good-bye, my youth.

It was a long time ago. I've been writing ever since with great care. I always hope the readers of my novels are of good quality. I wouldn't like to think of anyone cheap reading my books.

Edwina died at the age of ninety-eight. Her manservant Rudder had married Miss Fisher and they inherited her fortune.

Maisie Young opened a vegetarian restaurant which has flourished under the management of Beryl Tims.

Father Egbert Delaney was arrested in the park for exposing himself and then sent to a rehabilitation centre. Dottie, who is my chief informant on all these people, lost track of him after that.

Sir Eric Findlay died on good terms with his family, having lived long enough to earn the reputation of an eccentric rather than a nut.

The Baronne Clotilde du Loiret also died some time in the sixties, in California, where she had joined a highly organized religious sect. According to Dottie she died in the arms of her spiritual leader, an oriental mystic.

I have no idea whatsoever what happened to Mrs. Wilks.

But it is Solly Mendelsohn I mourn for. Solly, clumping and limping over Hampstead Heath with his large, night-pale face. Oh, Solly, my friend, my friend.

Dottie has been divorced and married so many

times I forget what her name is now. I live in Paris; and Dottie's present husband who is a journalist brought her to Paris a few years ago. She has problems with her children. She has the ugliest grandchild I have ever seen but she loves it. Dottie, under stress, stands under my window late at night singing "Auld Lang Syne," a ditty that the French fail to relish at one twenty-five in the morning.

The other day when I had looked in on Dottie, in her little flat, and had a row with her on the subject of my wriggling out of real life, unlike herself, I came out into the court-yard exasperated as usual. Some small boys were playing football, and the ball came flying straight towards me. I kicked it with a chance grace, which, if I had studied the affair and tried hard, I never could have done. Away into the air it went, and landed in the small boy's waiting hands. The boy grinned. And so, having entered the fullness of my years, from there by the grace of God I go on my way rejoicing.